UNWANTED WITNESS

Edmund Bradley, archivist at the University of Deniston is found murdered in his office. His expected visitor cannot be found, nor can Dr. Lewis Peel, with whom Bradley had quarrelled. Investigating, Hallam and Spratt confront missing 'top secret' papers and a second murder. The scene shifts to London, to a nursing home and a cremation at Golders Green. The mystery is unravelled when a crippled student determines to overcome his handicap by engaging in a forbidden climb of the university clock tower.

GEORGE DOUGLAS

UNWANTED WITNESS

Complete and Unabridged

LINFORD
Leicester

First published in Great Britain by
Robert Hale Limited
London

First Linford Edition
published 2006
by arrangement with
Robert Hale Limited
London

British Library CIP Data

Douglas, George
    Unwanted witness.—Large print ed.—
Linford mystery library
    1. Detective and mystery stories
    2. Large type books
    I. Title
    823.9'14 [F]

    ISBN 1-84617-259-4

Published by
F. A. Thorpe (Publishing)
Anstey, Leicestershire

Set by Words & Graphics Ltd.
Anstey, Leicestershire
Printed and bound in Great Britain by
T. J. International Ltd., Padstow, Cornwall

This book is printed on acid-free paper

ONE FOR AMY

1

The two police cars swung out of the main traffic rush into the quieter confines of Archer Row. The driver of the leading car, Detective Sergeant 'Jack' Spratt, of the Deniston C.I.D., spared a quick glance to left and right.

'Knew this district like my own backyard once,' he grunted. 'I was on a beat here. But that was before Higher Education took over with such power.'

Detective Chief Inspector William Hallam, seated beside him, looked with interest at the forest of scaffolding, the ponderous excavators, the jib cranes and the purposeful army of men, all cogs of the great machine which was crushing a former residential area into oblivion to make room for the expansion programme of the University of Deniston. Here and there, curtailed blocks of terrace houses, now converted into temporary university departments, still stood, and it was one of

1

these blocks to which Spratt directed the car.

He drew up in front of 2, Penn Road where a patrol-car constable stood with his back to a brown-painted door. There was a board on the wall alongside; 'University of Deniston, Department of Historical Research.' Hallam, tall, lean and lantern-jawed, got out of the car and returned the patrolman's greeting.

'First floor, sir, straight up the stairs. Etches is there, keeping an eye on things.'

'Right, Harrison.' Hallam turned back to the second 'I'll let you chaps know when I'm ready for you. We shouldn't be long.'

He and Spratt went through the door which Harrison's large hand shoved open for them. They stepped into a small entrance hall, with a room on either side, a passage leading to the rear of the house and a flight of stairs facing them. From beyond the turn of the stairs came a commotion of voices.

They went briskly up and came to a square landing from which four doors and a further flight of stairs opened off.

An elderly woman was seated in a chair, rocking back and forth and moaning shrilly, while a tall, thin man patted her shoulder ineffectively. Harrison's mate, Police Constable Etches sprang to attention as the detectives appeared. But as he opened his mouth to speak a young woman, attractive and brunette, came bustling out of one of the rooms carrying a cup of tea.

'Here you are, Mrs. Peachey!' She thrust the cup at the seated woman. 'Drink this and pull yourself together.' She looked inquiringly at Hallam. He introduced himself and Spratt.

'Good!' the young woman said. 'I'm Susan Howe, departmental secretary, and this is Mr. Clift, one of our lecturers.' The thin man ceased his ministrations and bestowed a nod each upon Hallam and Spratt. 'Mrs. Peachy here,' Miss Howe went on, 'is one of our cleaners. She found poor Mr. Bradley.'

'And never shall I forget it to me dying day! In I goes — '

'That's quite enough, dear!' Miss Howe said firmly. 'Drink your nice tea and I'll take you across to the rest room. You'll feel better in no time.'

Hallam turned to Etches, raising his eyebrows.

'In here, sir.' A thumb indicated a door, lettered, 'Institute of Regional History. Library and Archives.' Hallam pushed it open with his shoulder and went in, with Spratt at his heels. The sergeant closed the door and they stood there, side by side, their eyes busy.

It was a medium-sized room with a large window. Against one wall were sectional bookcases, filled and neatly labelled. Another wall accommodated tall metal filing cabinets. There was a cupboard in one corner and a long narrow table took up most of the centre space. At right-angles to this, set to catch the light, was a flat-topped wooden desk with a leather-padded tubular steel chair. The body of a grey-haired man was slumped in the chair, his head and chest supported by the desk, his arms dangling floorwards. From where they stood they could see how he had died, for the back of his skull was crushed and bloody.

'Yes,' Hallam said thoughtfully after a long pause. 'Not a nice thing to stumble on unexpectedly. Looks like the weapon on the floor there.'

Spratt went forward and squatted to examine a heavy electric iron with a rectangular base, its polished surface dulled and bespattered.

'Right,' Hallam said, when a quick search of the room had revealed nothing else of obvious importance. 'Tell Etches to bring the scientists up, will you, Jack? We'll get some details while they're busy.'

They returned to the landing. The two women had gone but Clift, the lecturer, was still standing irresolutely there. He started forward.

'This is a terrible thing, Chief Inspector — '

'Yes, sir.' Hallam spoke as Etches' heavy boots went clattering down the stairs. 'Is there somewhere where we can talk?'

'Of course. My room here.' He opened a door which was lettered with his name. 'I'll do all I can. Professor Kirk is the departmental head, but he hasn't come in

5

this morning yet.'

Clift's room had a large desk, and another long table, with wooden chairs pushed in under its edges. Spratt drew one of these out and sat down, opening his notebook. Somewhat fussily, Clift seated himself at his desk. Hallam crossed the room and leant against the mantelpiece.

'The police surgeon will be here at any moment, sir, though I'm afraid there's nothing he can do. My photographers and fingerprint men are setting to work in there now. Meanwhile, what can you tell me? Let's begin with the — er — victim.'

Clift put his elbows on his desk and steepled his fingers.

'His name is Bradley. Edward, or maybe Edgar, I really don't know. He works here as our librarian and archivist.' He noted Hallam's questioning look. 'Let me explain.

'This is a branch of the Faculty of Arts which specializes in regional history. Local history, if you prefer that label. We gather together, from parish records, private documents, from our field-workers and research people, all that type

6

of material which does not appear in the standard history texts.'

'And Mr. Bradley, sir?' Hallam prompted.

'Is — was — our archivist and librarian. It was his work to catalogue and file all accessions as they came in, in documentary form, as offprints of published material, as photographs. He has been with us — oh, nearly two years.'

'Thank you, sir. You've sketched in the background for us. Now, about this morning?'

'I can tell you very little. I arrived here just after nine. On my way from the car park I caught up with Miss Howe, who had called in at the main office for the mail. We came in here together and found the cleaner, Mrs. Peachey, in a state of collapse on the landing outside. When I understood what was amiss I went into Bradley's room.' He shuddered and his steepled fingertips whitened. 'I took a pull on myself, told Susan — Miss Howe — what had happened and instructed her to ring the police. Your men were here very promptly.' He frowned. 'Bradley must have been . . . there . . . all night.

His hours are from nine-thirty to four-thirty.'

The rattle of a typewriter from beyond the wall of the room rose, continued and ceased. Hallam caught Spratt's eye as the sergeant looked up from his shorthand notes.

'Yes, sergeant?'

'That iron, sir. Obviously the instrument used. How did that come to be there?'

'Oh, yes,' Clift said. 'Quite simple. Part of Bradley's job was to mount and file photographs. We use the dry-mounting process. A piece of specially-prepared tissue is cut to the size of the print. An application of the hot iron, which is smoothed over the print face, causes the picture to adhere firmly to the card on which it is mounted.'

Spratt thanked him and conscientiously noted the information in his book. Hallam cleared his throat.

'Now, sir. Had Bradley any enemies, to your knowledge?'

'None, as far as I am aware. He was a quiet, rather self-effacing person. He did his work competently and fitted in extremely well here. I know Professor Kirk will agree with me that . . . ' His mouth tightened, his words trailed off.

'Yes, sir?' Hallam prompted.

'Bradley did step out of line once. About six months ago. He took it upon himself to attack Dr. Peel, of the Faculty of Science here, in the columns of the students' weekly newspaper. Peel is a metallurgist and I understand his particular field is metal fatigue. Bradley, apparently a member of the International Peace Union, got it into his mind that Peel was working on — er — aggressive missiles. Peel, of course, was furious when the article was brought to his notice and came storming down here to have it out with Bradley. Fortunately, Professor Kirk was able to pour some oil on the troubled waters though Bradley refused to make a public apology in the paper and Peel demanded his resignation from the staff here.' He grimaced. 'A nasty business all round while it lasted. It was the Vice Chancellor himself who persuaded Peel to forget the whole thing and, of course,

Kirk wouldn't hear of Bradley resigning.'

There was a knock at the door and Spratt rose to answer it. He turned back into the room and spoke to Hallam.

'Dr. Ransome, sir. Just finished. Can you spare a moment?'

Hallam said, 'Excuse us, sir,' and went out with Spratt to the landing. The police surgeon, his usual dapper and fresh-looking self, greeted him cheerfully.

'Morning, Hallam! Appears quite open-and-shut, this one. Been dead something like twelve hours, I'd say, but I'd better have him on the table before I put any-thing into writing. Bung him along, will you, as soon as your snapshot boys have finished?'

He waved airily and hurried off. Hallam stepped into the archives room, to be greeted by a blinding flash of magnesium flare.

'And that's the lot,' the photographer said, lowering his camera. 'Got your sketches finished, Brian?'

His assistant nodded.

'Get busy chalking round him, then, and we'll be on our way. There's nothing else, is there, sir?'

'I don't think so.' Hallam spoke to the finger-print men who were dusting and blowing busily. 'Any luck with that iron?'

'Wiped clean, sir. Every inch of it. Somebody did a good job on that.'

Hallam shrugged and spoke to Spratt. 'Pockets, Jack, then.' He gave Etches orders to call up the mortuary van and, returning to Clift's room, found the lecturer fiddling aimlessly with papers on his desk.

'I think, sir, I'll have a word with your secretary next.'

'Of course.' Clift pushed a button on his desk. 'Susan usually has all the answers, but in this case . . . ' He shrugged dismally.

Miss Howe came nimbly in and seated herself neatly with her feet together and her hands in her lap.

'There's just one point first, Chief Inspector,' Clift said. 'This dreadful business is going to disrupt our work here completely. I feel I should be making some immediate arrangements.'

Susan Howe smiled briefly. 'I've attended

to that, Mr. Clift. I've pinned a notice on the front door to say all lectures, tutorials and seminars are cancelled until further notice. I also rang Prof. Kirk at the City Records Office where he has an appointment this morning. I gave him the news and he'll be along here as soon as he can.' She turned to Hallam, ready now for questioning.

'I was about to ask Mr. Clift, when I was called away just now, when he had last seen Mr. Bradley alive, Miss Howe. I shall have to put the same question to you.'

Clift answered without hesitation.

'Yesterday afternoon, just before three. I was on my way to a Faculty meeting in the main Arts Building and stepped into his room to return a book I had taken from the library.'

'And you, Miss Howe?'

'I took him in a cup of tea about half-past three. I didn't actually see him again. He leaves at four-thirty and I work till five. As usual, when he left he called out good-bye to me — I was in my office with the door partly open. I heard him go down the stairs. On my own way out, later, I tried the door of his room, to check it was locked.' She glanced sideways to give Spratt a brief smile as he came into the room, carrying a bulging manilla envelope. 'You see, some little time ago a set of keys to these rooms was lost, and one morning an expensive camera and some money were missing, so since then we've taken extra care to see everything locked up before we leave.'

Hallam, now in the chair Spratt had used, sat forward. 'We'd better hear more about this.'

Clift roused himself to answer.

'Each of us — Professor Kirk, Miss Howe, Bradley and myself had keys, for the front door of this house and for our own rooms. The room locks are all alike, I mean, my key, for instance, will open any of the other doors on this floor. The arrangement is for the convenience of the cleaners, who come in early and also have a set of two keys, for the outer door and for these rooms. About six weeks ago the cleaners' keys were lost — just how, was a mystery never cleared up. Some ten days

13

afterwards my room was entered one night. The camera, which I had been checking before issuing it on loan to one of our post-graduate field workers, was taken from a drawer here.' He tapped his desk. 'Also money, eleven pounds ten in notes. I am the Senior Common Room treasurer and had been collecting members' subscriptions. The desk drawers had been forced. I have had new locks fitted since.'

'The theft was reported to us, sir?'

Clift exchanged a glance with the secretary. 'Well, no.' He spoke uncomfortably. 'You see, Chief Inspector, in a community like this — a modern university anxious to build up and maintain a sound public image — adverse publicity is avoided wherever possible. One doesn't rush these things. And meanwhile, within forty-eight hours of the discovery of the theft, the camera and the notes were returned, all intact. They were parcelled up, addressed to me and placed on the floor outside my door here. The security guard found the parcel on his night round. The odd thing was that the missing keys were enclosed in the parcel also.'

'You were lucky, sir.'

Clift shrugged. 'Obviously, a student's idea of a joke, Chief Inspector. Quite pointless, but then, most students' jokes and raggings are.'

Hallam dropped the subject. 'How is your security guard system worked here, sir?'

'I'm afraid I'm not very clear about that.' Clift looked again at Susan Howe. She answered readily.

'The guards make rounds at night. But we never see them, so I can't tell you who does this block of houses. The head porter in the main building would know, of course. I can ring him if you like.'

'Thank you, Miss Howe, but we'll see him personally. Now, we'll need Mr. Bradley's private address.'

'I've already looked it up for you.' Again she turned to Spratt. '2a Westwood Court, Park Road. It's a flat. Mr. Bradley wasn't married.'

'So he left at his usual time yesterday,' Hallam summarized, 'and must have returned later. Was this a custom of his, do you know?'

Both Clift and Susan shook their heads. 'I'd no idea he'd do such a thing,' the secretary said. 'I mean, he wasn't worked hard here, was he, Mr. Clift? It wasn't as though he wanted to deal with stuff which had piled up. In fact, he often used to say he wished he'd more to do during the day.'

Hallam pushed back his chair. 'Well, if Mrs. Peachy is feeling better now, perhaps we can have a word with her.'

'I'll ask her to come up.' Susan jumped up briskly and then paused, listening to sounds on the landing outside. A man's voice rose in sharp reproof.

'Watch it, can't yer, Charlie? You'll have him off the bloody stretcher in a minute! Damn it, the poor bloke's suffered enough without getting chucked base over apex down these stairs!'

It was Spratt who noticed Susan Howe's sudden glassy-eyed stare. He caught her as she was falling, lowered her gently into a chair and pressed her head downwards. Clift sprang up.

'I'll get a glass of water! I don't wonder, poor girl! Such a terrible business!'

'Delayed shock, sir,' Hallam said. 'And I'd just hang on here a minute or two, if I were you, till the ambulance people get clear.'

Susan struggled, shook her head and sat up.

'Stupid of me,' she murmured. 'I don't usually . . .'

'You must go home and rest,' Clift said. 'Never mind the work here today. I'll bring my car round.'

'Good idea, sir,' Hallam agreed. He motioned to Spratt who, picking up the large envelope, followed him out. Hallam touched the envelope.

'Anything promising here, Jack?'

'I don't think so, sir. I haven't had a chance to examine the items in detail but there's nothing unusual.'

In the archivist's room the finger-print men were packing up their kit.

'We'll get these sorted, quick as we can, sir,' the senior man promised. 'There's less than you'd expect, seems to me the cleaners did a good job on this place every day. What about this iron? There's nothing obvious on it, but I'd like to have another go at it in the lab. We've found the cardboard box which usually holds it.'

'Right. Let Dr. Ransome know you've got it, will you? He'll probably want to make a comparison.'

Three minutes later Hallam and Spratt were alone in the house. Clift and Susan had gone, Etches and his mate had been sent back to their normal patrol, with instructions from Hallam to request, on their car radio, a uniformed man to be posted at the entrance. Mutually avoiding the chair at the still-stained desk, they perched sideways on the long table on which Spratt emptied the contents of his envelope.

As the sergeant had said, it appeared a normal collection. Handkerchief, four Yale keys on a stout ring, pocket-knife, wallet, notecase, a biro pen, a pocket diary, loose change.

'Non-smoker,' Hallam commented. He picked up the wallet and began to take out its contents. Spratt flicked the notecase open, found two pound notes in it, put it aside and tried the diary.

'Membership cards for a golf club and a photographic society,' Hallam mused aloud. 'Couple of business letters, book of stamps, four receipted bills. He slipped his fingers inside the back compartment which ran the length of the wallet, removed a folded sheet of paper and opened it out.

'Funny,' Spratt said suddenly. 'He used this diary for odd notes only.'

'And what's funny about that?'

'This entry under yesterday's date. A name and a time — nine-thirty. It's the name that's odd. Humpkin.'

Hallam pushed over the paper he was holding.

'Take a look at this, too.'

There were words in a rough scrawl, with a date ten days previously. 'I.O.U. five hundred pounds.' The signature was almost illegible and as Spratt tilted it to the light, footsteps sounded on the landing outside. The door opened and a very short, very fat, very bald middle-aged man bounced into the room.

2

'Hi!' he greeted. 'You'll be the C.I.D., what? I'm Ken Kirk. This is proper nauseating, isn't it? Tell me all — there doesn't seem to be anybody else around to spill the lowdown.'

'Professor Kirk? The head of this department?' Hallam asked.

'Yeaup. Secretary Sue buzzed me. I put the skids under myself at the earliest possible.'

'Detective Chief Inspector Hallam, sir. And Detective Sergeant Spratt.'

The bald head jerked at each of them in turn.

'This I can't get with, Hallam.' His glance fastened on the stained desk, then slid away. 'They tell me poor old Bradley was killed. Head bashed in. But, hell's bells, who'd do a thing like that?'

'That's what we've to find out, sir. We've only just made a start, of course. We've talked to Mr. Clift and Miss Howe

— the business upset her badly and Mr. Clift has taken her home. They weren't able to help much.'

Kirk raised his heavy shoulders. 'Same here, I'm afraid. I haven't the faintest. Of course — let's admit it — I didn't know him really well. Outside of here, I mean, if you get me. I appointed the old lad, of course. I judged him the type I needed as an archivist and he sure proved that bet copper-bottomed.'

Hallam signed to Spratt, who gathered up the small heap on the table and shovelled its items into the envelope.

'We haven't had time yet to look over the building, sir. Perhaps you'd be good enough . . . ?'

'Why, sure!' He dug out keys from a trousers pocket. 'Two rooms downstairs which are open during the day for the lads and lassies to use as study rooms. Up here, the office, Clift's pied-à-terre and my own cubby-hole. On the floor above, a collection of small dark spots — servants slept there once, no doubt — mostly empty, a couple used as store-rooms. Let us away.'

Their tour was brief and completely unrewarding. Kirk ended it by taking them into his own room, a slightly larger edition of Clift's, with a carpet on the floor over the brown linoleum. He waved them to chairs, perching himself on a corner of a large, untidily-loaded desk. He took out a heavy pipe with a curved stem and as he stuffed it with tobacco from an oilskin pouch, Hallam studied him between narrowed lids. In spite of the man's outdated undergraduate slang, his obvious desire to be considered a 'character,' Hallam felt he was facing a very shrewd, very competent professor indeed.

Kirk lit a match and puffed mightily. From behind a dense cloud of acrid smoke he said, 'The door in the corner there. It communicates with the next house in this row, where the Medieval Historians live, move and have their wretched being. Fire precaution, you know, as there's only one exit from each house — the street door. I came in through Med. Hist. this morning. Saw your cop on duty on the steps downstairs and decided I wouldn't bother him by coming the direct way.'

'So this house could be entered from either of the front doors, sir?' Spratt asked.

'You said it, sarge. Given the said door was unlocked, or if you had the requisite key. As I told you just now, the rear entrance doors are kept double bolted inside. We never use 'em, anyway.'

He fanned smoke from in front of his face and immediately replaced it with a fresh cloud.

'So Gilbert Clift told you about the missing keys and the brouhaha we had here when old Gil's desk was bust into. Gil's not a bad lad, but we don't spill everything to him.'

'Meaning, sir?'

'When Gilbert Clift discovered the break-in — and a fine song and dance he made of it — he checked what was missing and then came at a rate of knots to me, demanding police action on the dot. Actually, I'd been ahead of him there. As soon as I first heard of it, I was about to dial you chaps on the blower here' — he nodded to the telephone on his desk — 'when poor Bradley came in and besought me, with some urgency, to stay my hand. He swore he would get the missing stuff returned within a day or two. He wouldn't say more, but he sold me on it. I unloaded a heap of old junk on Clift about the perils of publicity and the necessity of moving through the proper channels. Bradley's promise turned out gilt-edged. The stuff came back inside a couple of days.'

'You didn't suspect Bradley himself, sir?'

'Good grief, no! He was a keen amateur photographer and he'd at least two cameras much more fab than the one which went A.W.O.L. from this dump. And he wasn't at all short of the old mazuma. We didn't pay him much here, but when I offered to put in a claim for an increase for him he wouldn't have it. Said it would only mean more for the income-tax vultures. No, we got the stuff back and that was fair enough for me. Fine, as far as I was concerned.'

Hallam glanced at his watch and at

once felt a prickle of irritation. Time was moving on and it seemed they were getting nowhere.

'I understand Mr. Bradley was in some trouble recently with a Dr. Peel, of the Science Faculty, sir.'

Kirk nodded. 'Bad do, that. I had to bring out all the old tact I could muster. That's water under the bridge now, though.'

'I shall have to have a word with Dr. Peel, all the same.'

'Sure, sure. Like me to get the lad now?' Without waiting for Hallam's reply, Kirk picked up his telephone. 'Dr. Peel, please. Metallurgy.' He sat whistling softly through his teeth while the switchboard made his connection. Then, 'Hallo. Kenneth Kirk here. Regional History. Is Dr. Peel around? . . . I see. Right. No, no message — it'll do later. Thanks.' He cradled the instrument and primmed his lips. 'Peel's not there. They've had a call from his wife to say he won't be in for a day or two. He's away from home on some urgent private business.'

'Thank you, sir. That's one job we can

put off.' Hallam paused, sorting his thoughts into order. Spratt said, 'Excuse me, sir,' and was told to carry on. He tapped the envelope he was holding and spoke to Kirk.

'I've Mr. Bradley's diary here, sir. Under yesterday's date is a name — Humpkin. Does that mean anything to you?'

'Humpkin? Odd moniker, isn't it? No, never heard it before. It's nothing to do with his work here, I can tell you that.'

'There's a time with the name — nine-thirty. It seems possible that Mr. Bradley had an appointment — '

Spratt broke off as a hesitant knock sounded on the communicating door. Kirk glanced at Hallam and at the detective's nod called a hearty, 'Come in!'

The cleaner, Mrs. Peachy, sidled into the room, a long-handled brush in one hand, a duster in the other.

'Excuse me, sir' — she spoke to Kirk — 'but I was just going off duty and I thought, seeing as how I found the body, I reely ought to make sure first, like, that the detectives didn't want to ask me

26

anything, or like that.'

Hallam rose. 'You're feeling all right now, Mrs. Peachey?'

She bobbed at him. 'Oh, yes, sir. It were the shock, like.'

'Well, I don't think we've much to ask you. When you came in this morning, was the outer door locked?'

'It was, sir, like it allus is. I come in and dusted and brushed me way round, like. I allus leave Mr. Bradley — poor soul — till last, becos he's the end one, you see. I opened his door with me key and went in.' She swallowed painfully.

'Was the electric light on in that room?'

'It was, sir. First thing I noticed as I pushed the door open. Hullo, I thought, he's left it on since yesterday. And I switched it off as I went in, like. I hope I didn't do wrong, sir.'

'Oh, no, Mrs. Peachy, no harm done.'

She frowned. 'Come to think of it now, that was odd. He leaves by half-past four so why'd he have a light on, on a sunny afternoon? Which it was.'

'We think he came back later. That'll be all, and thank you.'

She bobbed her head again and withdrew. Kirk put his pipe down.

'Licks me why Bradley came back here last night. There was no reason, from the point of view of his job, I mean. What was that name again — the one in the diary? Humpkin. No, never heard of it. Look, I take it you'll be jazzing around the old department for quite a while yet? I mean, I'd like to know when we can trickle back to normal.'

'Probably by tomorrow, sir. I shall have to have a second, more detailed search made of your archives room. I'll send a man up to do that. Meanwhile, the room must not be entered.'

'Leave that to me. I'll be here all morning.' He sighed. 'I suppose I'd better let the top brass know what's happened. Poor old Brad! You could look about all day and never find a better bloke, Chief Inspector.'

'Epitaph on an archivist,' Hallam murmured as he and Spratt went downstairs. 'But it doesn't give us much light. We'll see the head porter now, Jack.'

He stopped for a word with the

constable on duty at the outer door and then followed Spratt to the car. Penn Road formed a short cut between the newer blocks of lecture rooms and the campus, around which the Students' Union building, the refectories and the main administration offices and library were situated. Hallam eased himself into the car beside his sergeant.

'What's young Howard doing this morning, Jack?'

'I sent him to St. Mary's. A chap got knocked down by a car in Harlow Street last night. The driver didn't stop. The chap was still unconscious this morning. Not a scrap of identity on him. I told Howard to get over to the hospital and see if he could ferret something out.'

Hallam picked up the car's radio telephone. He called Headquarters and gave instructions for Howard to be recalled from the hospital and sent to Penn Road. The constable on duty there would give him orders from Hallam.

Spratt switched on the car's engine, and they drove into the campus, a generously-designed square with a fountain and flower beds in its centre. A flight of wide steps led to the entrance of the main administration building.

Carr, the head porter, was an elderly man with a weary and cynical eye. His office had a long counter and a range of shelves at the back which held items of property waiting to be claimed by their careless owners. He sat on a high stool at one end of the counter, drinking tea from a thick blue mug. Hallam explained who they were and what had happened that morning in Penn Road. Carr whistled softly.

' 'Strewth! That's a turn up, if ever there was one.' He sipped tea noisily. 'And how can I help you, gentlemen?'

'We need a run-down on the night security arrangements here,' Hallam said. 'And we'll have to see the man who covered Penn Road last night.'

'Ah,' Carr replied. He put down his mug and, bending to a shelf below the counter, produced a ledger-sized book. 'Well, you must understand we head porters work a shift system. There's four of us. This place is never left unattended, day nor night. That makes forty-two hours a week for each of us. We do split shifts when we want to change from early, late and night turns. I come on at eight this morning when my mate Sam Handley went off. The night man is responsible for the security blokes, so Sam would . . . Ah, here we are.' He ran his finger down a page. 'Molloy, he did Penn Road last night. He went off at eight, too, so you might catch him still up if you was to go now. 63 Jackman Street. That's out by the Rovers' ground. He's in lodgings there.'

A cross-town route brought them, a quarter of an hour later, into a small estate of new corporation-built houses which had risen on the site of a slum-demolition area. An elderly Ford Popular stood outside 63 Jackman Street and the house door was opened to them by a handsome dark-haired man in his early thirties. He wore a collarless blue shirt and dark Melton-cloth trousers over carpet slippers.

'Sure, I'm Patrick Molloy,' he admitted

cheerfully. 'Police, is it, now? Ye'll step inside, then. The landlady's out at the shops. We can talk in peace here.'

He showed them into a front room, well-furnished and spotlessly kept. He found them chairs and stood on the hearthrug facing them. 'And what can I be doing for ye?'

Briefly, Hallam gave him the facts of Bradley's death. Molloy's blue eyes widened.

'God rest his soul, the poor man! Murder, was it?'

'We'll call it homicide for the moment, Mr. Molloy. You knew Mr. Bradley, then?'

'Och, I never set eyes on the man at all, now. Why would I be doing that, when he'd be working in the day time and me a night guard?'

'Of course. Well, now. You were on the Penn Road beat last night. Anything unusual there?'

Molloy thrust his hands deep into his trousers pockets. His blue eyes were lidded in thought.

'We report for duty at eight. There's usually still a lot going on then, evening lectures the public go to, often people working late in their rooms. We just wander about for an hour, letting people see we're on the job, like. And then we knock off for a smoke and a cup of tay in the security staffroom. Sure, it'll be ten o'clock or near by when we get off on our beats. Me own round takes ninety minutes, done slow and proper. Seeing all's well, ye know, no fires, doors locked. We're back having our suppers be midnight. And then two more rounds before six or turned.'

'And last night?' Hallam repeated.

'Not a thing out of place, sorr. Sure I went into the Penn Road houses, all the three times, and divil a sight or sound that shouldn't be.'

'Just tell me exactly what you did when you checked Number Two, Penn Road, Mr. Molloy.'

'Now, then . . . I let meself in by the front door. I turned on the bottom light and checked the rooms below were locked. I switched the landing light on, climbed the stairs, tried the room doors there. Ivery wan fast, I can swear to it.

Then up to the attic floor and all well there. I put the lights out, locked the front door and went on to the next house.'

'And you did exactly the same on your other two visits?'

'I did, then. Except the third time — 'twould be around five this morning — I didn't go up to the attic floor. I was a bit behind me schedule.'

'Did you notice the light was on in the archives room?'

The blue eyes widened now. 'I did not. I wouldn't be seeing it, anyway, with the landing light on and the door fast.'

'Of course not.' Hallam paused and then asked,

'What part of Ireland are you from, Mr. Molloy?'

'From Dublin. I came over here with the idea of getting into the building trade but I saw this advert for the university job and they took me on. I'm a bit of a judo expert, ye know, and I've played rugby. Me references was gone into and they stood up all right.'

Hallam got up. 'We won't keep you any longer, Mr. Molloy. You're absolutely dead certain you didn't see anything out of the ordinary last night?'

'I did not, sorr. And, sure, I wish I had.'

'And the next thing, sir?' Spratt asked as they returned to their car.

'Bradley's flat, I fancy. You have the address.'

Spratt opened his notebook. '2a Westwood Court, Park Road. If I cut across City Centre and take the road out to Gray's Avenue — yes, that's it.'

Westwood Court had begun its existence as the town residence of one of Deniston's engineering magnates in the days when Deniston-made machinery was supreme throughout the civilized world. It was situated off a pleasant, tree-lined road, and its front approach was still gracefully attractive. Three storeys and a basement, Hallam noted as the car swung into the forecourt. Say six flats, plus caretaker. Fairly expensive, but not modern enough to be priced sky-high.

In the portico Spratt found a labelled bank of bell-pushes. He pressed the one marked 'Atkinson, Caretaker,' and was about to ring again when steps sounded within and the door was opened by a dark-haired, still-handsome woman of middle age. She gave them a token smile and said, 'Yes?' in a voice whose impatience she made no attempt to conceal.

But when Hallam had explained their business, all irritation at an interrupted morning vanished. Mrs. Atkinson was almost dumb with shock. 'I — ' she said, and 'Well, I simply can't — I mean, Mr. Bradley — I can't — '

'Take it easy, Mrs. Atkinson,' Hallam advised her gently. 'Now, look. I know you're upset over this, but we've our job to do. That entails asking you a few questions and having a look at Mr. Bradley's rooms. All right?'

She nodded. 'Shall we go downstairs first? I was just making coffee. Perhaps you would let me offer you some?'

The familiar routine of coffee-making and carrying a tray into a sitting-room which had once been a basement kitchen, brought Mrs. Atkinson back to normal. She waited until Hallam and Spratt were settled with cups in their hands and then leant forward.

'My husband and I have lived here as caretakers for the past three years. Mr. Bradley was one of our oldest residents, and had been here for some ten years, I think. He was quiet, never any trouble and a general favourite. Sometimes he'd bring a friend in to stay the night, but this was only very occasionally. But something very odd happened about a month ago and I think I should tell you about it.'

'Please do, Mrs. Atkinson.'

'Mr. Bradley's rooms are on the first floor. Opposite him is Miss Fenn. She had been away visiting her sister and was due back that particular evening. I went up about seven o'clock to put hot water bottles in her bed. I couldn't help hearing that Mr. Bradley had a visitor and that there was a terrific row going on in his sitting-room. At least, somebody — a man — was shouting at Mr. Bradley. I heard him say, 'If you do, I'll get you for it, Bradley, if it's my last act.' Then Mr. Bradley, quieter, as if he were trying to calm the other man down. He said, 'Pull yourself together, Malcolm, and listen to me.' At that I went into Miss Fenn's flat and heard no more. But as I came out Mr. Bradley was standing at his door and a man was just disappearing downstairs. Mr. Bradley sort of shrugged his shoulders and said: 'These students, Mrs. Atkinson! They will go off at half-cock!' And that was the end of it as far as I was concerned.'

'Could you identify this visitor, Mrs. Atkinson?'

'Oh, no. I only got a glimpse of his back. I think he had darkish hair and he was fairly tall.'

'But you're certain you heard the name Malcolm?'

'Quite certain. I have a brother Malcolm, so it stuck in my mind. If you've finished your coffee, I'll take you up to Mr. Bradley's flat.'

3

Detective Constable Arthur Howard, recently transferred to C.I.D., stood in an ante-room off Ward Eighteen in St. Mary's Hospital, turning over, for the third time, the heap of clothes and personal items on the table in front of him.

Sergeant Spratt had put him on this assignment. It had seemed simple enough — to discover the identity of a man who had been knocked down by a car in Heron Road the previous evening. But a brass-faced ward sister had viewed his appearance with extreme disfavour and had practically ordered him off the premises. The patient was not conscious, she had said icily, and was likely to remain in that state for a considerable period, even possibly a matter of days. There was no point in the police hanging about and getting in the way of her staff.

His official dignity, still in a tender

stage, grossly affronted, Howard had insisted on waiting to see the doctor in charge of the ward cases. 'Then you'll have time on your hands,' the sister told him tartly. 'Dr. Soper is not likely to be making his rounds until later this morning.' That set Howard a poser — should he hang on here or report back to H.Q.? Just in time he remembered to ask for the patient's clothes and personal effects. He had them listed in his notebook now, but as for identification, there just wasn't any.

A cheap off-the-peg suit, popular makes in under-clothes and shoes. The pockets had contained a handkerchief, small change and a roll of digestive tablets. There was a wallet which held six pound notes, and a card of Yorkshire Cricket Club fixtures. No driving licence, receipts, photographs nor membership cards. He checked the lot again and wished he could decide whether to go or stay.

The door of the ante-room opened and a probationer nurse came in.

'There's a phone call for you, love.'

In the ward, at the sister's table, Howard picked up the telephone.

'C.I.D. Headquarters,' the receiver said impersonally. 'I have a message for you from Detective Chief Inspector Hallam. You are to proceed at once to the university, to a house at 2 Penn Road, where the constable on duty will give you further instructions. Acknowledge, please.'

Howard found Penn Road without too much trouble, and replied to the constable's bland inquiry as to where the 'ell he'd been all day by shrugging his shoulders and muttering, 'Rushed to death. That's C.I.D. all over. Never a minute's peace.'

'I'll change you jobs,' the constable offered. 'I'm fed-up of standing here, taking a load of mickey from that gang on the demolition job yonder. You've to go upstairs, first floor, and search a room where a bloke had his skull bashed in this morning.'

On the first floor Howard heard a murmur of voices behind a door marked 'Professor K. Kirk.' He knocked and was bidden to enter.

In five minutes he had all the details he needed from Professor Kirk, seconded by Clift, who had returned from seeing Susan Howe home. He took the key Kirk gave him, went into the archives room and closed the door behind him.

The rusty-brown splotches on the desk top brought a grimace to his handsome young face, but he set to work at once. There were three drawers at one side of the desk, none on the other. He pulled out the top drawer. It held pencils, a wooden ruler, a pair of scissors and several note-books. Howard turned the pages of these and found they were concerned only with Bradley's job.

The second drawer housed an automatic numerator in a cardboard box, departmental-headed notepaper, envelopes, a duster and a book of stamps. The lowest drawer was full of official correspondence and circular letters addressed to members of the academic staff. Not a single clue there.

At one side of the room were two tall metal filing cabinets.

The nearer of the two contained four

deep drawers. Three of these were filled with metal-edged files, hooked to runners. The files were labelled and held photographs of historical interest. In the lowest drawer Howard found a collection of cut cardboard and several packets of the dry mounting tissue for the photographs. There were also wrapped packets of variously-coloured file cards, which, he found, fitted the compartments of the second large cabinet. Here in a dozen shallow drawers, labelled by subject, were cards containing items of regional history.

He pulled out each drawer in turn, giving its contents a casual glance. In one of them a torn piece of paper stuck out above the neatly-stacked cards, as though a card had been removed for reference and the paper was there to mark the place. Howard removed the paper. It bore a pencilled scrawl, 'Humpkin. Old house in Dales.' Since it was the only out-of-place feature he had lighted upon, he placed it between the pages of his notebook.

He glanced along the shelves of the library unit, and was gazing through the window from where he could glimpse, between two high buildings, a narrow view of the campus, restless with hurrying figures, when the street door opened and shut and quick footsteps ascended the stairs. The door of the room in which he stood was thrust open and Sergeant Spratt stepped in.

'Now, then, lad. Found anything?'

'Nothing, sarge. And I've been through everything except the library books. By the way, the chap at the hospital's still badly concussed. He might be that way for days, they think. And absolutely no identification either from his clothes or the contents of his pockets.'

'Ah, well, never mind him now.' Spratt's head was turning from side to side. 'You're sure you've examined everything — any letters, scraps of paper, all that?'

'Everything, sarge. Including the files. The only thing out of place was this.' For what it was worth, he produced the torn paper he had taken from the card file.

He was completely unprepared for his sergeant's reaction. Spratt glanced at the scrap, looked again and emitted a choked sound which was half-way between surprise and triumph.

'Humpkin!' he said. 'Same as in his diary. What's this? Old house in Dales? Might mean anything. Old house — historical, no doubt. Show me where you found this.'

Howard did so. He'd made a mental note of the cards the paper had separated.

'Tells us nothing,' Spratt grunted. He leant against the window sill. 'You'd better get the outline of this job. You'll have work to do on it. Now, listen.'

He related the facts crisply. 'Mr. Hallam and I did a search of Bradley's flat,' he concluded, 'and got practically nothing. From what he told the caretaker, he had no relations at all. As far as I can see we've three lines of inquiry — no, four. There's the I.O.U. we found in his wallet — the signature seems to be Crayston. We found a cheque stub of the date previous to that on the I.O.U. drawn to self for £500. There's the row he had here with Dr. Peel, the one he had with this Malcolm chap at his flat, and there's

Humpkin, when we can find him, who he was apparently meeting at nine-thirty. That must have been last night.'

'Yes, sergeant.'

'We can't do anything about Peel at the moment,' Spratt continued, 'because he's away from home. Humpkin we may be able to contact through the phone directory or the electoral rolls. So we'll have a go at Crayston and this Malcolm chap. Crayston may be somewhere in the university, we know Malcolm is a student here. Let's go.'

They dropped the Yale lock of the archives room and crossed the landing. Kirk's voice called them in.

'Ah, sergeant!' he said. 'Jolly glad you toddled by again. Look, I've had to report this, of course, to the brass. And has it fluttered the dovecotes, or has it? But you mustn't bear down on me because of the hell of a splash there'll be in the evening rag tonight.'

'Not to worry, sir. Chief Inspector Hallam will be dealing with the Press right now. A couple more names have turned up. Crayston and Malcolm. Can you help us?'

Clift answered at once. 'We have a second-year student named Crayston. He isn't due to attend at this department today, but he'll be somewhere around the place. Our central admin. people would have a copy of his time-table. You could locate him by that.'

'And Malcolm?'

Both men shook their heads. 'Christian name, is it?' Kirk asked.

'We imagine so. Perhaps your administration office — ?'

'I've no doubt about it, sergeant.'

'Then we'll get on to it now. If you'd be good enough to direct us.'

They found the main office of the Department of History in a temporary wooden building set between the two newly-finished blocks of Agriculture and Psychology. A clerk at the inquiry counter thought they had better see Miss Porter. 'She's chief admin.,' the girl added, and directed them along a passage.

If Miss Porter had donned a cap and a stiffly-starched apron and cuffs, Howard thought, she'd be a dead ringer for that hospital sister. She had the same no-nonsense manner, the same gimlet eyes.

'News has already reached me of the tragedy,' she said flatly. 'I am, of course, very sorry. Now, if you'll tell me exactly what it is you want, I've no doubt I can help you.' She helped them to the extent of pressing a bell which summoned a cheerful, auburn-haired young woman.

'Mrs. Hopkins will attend to you,' she said. 'Good morning.'

Mrs. Hopkins took them back to the main office, found a folder in a filing cabinet, removed a cyclostyled form from it and ran a rose-tipped finger along a line.

'Walter John Crayston,' she said. 'If he hasn't cut it, he'll be at Mr. Whiteford's lecture now.' She glanced at her watch. 'It's due to finish in five minutes. Would you like me to take you across? Then you can catch Crayston as he comes out.'

She took them across the campus to another huge block. 'Arts Building,' she said and led the way to a lift. They got out at the second floor and followed her down a corridor to a door above which was an illuminated sign — 'Lecture Proceeding.'

48

'Just in time,' she said. From within came the scraping of chairs on the floor, a rising buzz of talk. The door opened and a small, grey-haired man came hurrying out and trotted towards the lift, his gown swinging. At his heels poured a crowd of young men and women. Mrs. Hopkins stepped forward into the mob and touched a tall, fair-haired young man on the shoulder.

'Just a moment, Mr. Crayston, please.'

He turned sharply, and so did the slim, pretty girl with him.

'Oh, hullo! What's the trouble?' He looked frowningly at Howard and Spratt.

'These gentlemen would like a word with you.' Mrs. Hopkins stepped back. 'I'll go and look up that other name,' she told Spratt. 'Call in at the office again, will you?'

Spratt nodded. The crowd was thinning rapidly now.

'Police. C.I.D.,' he said to Crayston. 'Is there somewhere we can talk to you?'

'To me?' His frown deepened.

'Just a brief inquiry, sir. Shouldn't take long.'

'We'd better go inside, then.' He jerked a thumb at the room he had just left. 'Morning lectures are over now so we'll be quite private.' He put a hand on the girl's arm. 'Hang on a minute, will you, Val?'

Her face had gone white and she nodded dumbly, walking slowly away along the corridor. Crayston gestured to the detectives and followed them into the lecture room. He leaned against the tall desk in front of the wall blackboard.

'What is all this, then?'

'You are acquainted with Mr. Bradley, sir?'

They saw his mouth tighten.

'The archivist bloke at Regional History? Of course. Reg. Hist. is one of my subsiduary subjects. I use the archives now and then. So what?'

'Mr. Bradley was killed in his office last night, sir. He was struck with the iron he used for mounting photographs.'

Crayston's eyes and mouth opened. 'He — what?'

'I'm stating a fact, sir.'

'But . . . You mean he was done in?'

Crayston seemed to be fighting for self-control. He swallowed painfully and said, in a high, near-hysterical voice, 'I'm sorry. Very sorry. He was a decent old boy. I mean, he never blew his top if you kept one of his library books out too long. And — and so on,' he finished lamely.

Spratt bore on, like a boxer keen to finish his rubber-legged opponent before the bell for the end of the round.

'You owed him money, I believe. A matter of £500.'

Crayston dragged in a short, noisy breath and his eyes flashed defiance. But only for a moment. Quite suddenly, he crumpled against the desk, licking his lips.

'All right, then. So I did. But I didn't ask him for the loan. He offered it me.'

Spratt relaxed. 'Right, sir. Tell us the whole tale.'

'I'd been living it up,' Crayston said. 'I dunno — this university life seemed to go to my head. It wasn't so bad last year, my first, but I hadn't met Valerie then.' He jerked a hand in the direction of the corridor outside. 'I rather fell, you see, and she was very popular. I had to make a show for her. So I bought this car, and threw a few parties and — oh, other stupidities and I was deep in the red before I could look around.

'Tradesmen and other people began to threaten and I couldn't go to my parents. They aren't at all well off. I didn't know what to do, so I asked Mr. Bradley's advice. He was that sort — you could talk to him. And he said he'd lend me the money.'

He licked his lips again.

'He drew the cash from his bank and handed it over the following day. That would be — oh, about ten days ago. He gave me a piece of blank paper, I made out an I.O.U. and he put it in his wallet and said there was no hurry about repaying the money. But I've got nearly two hundred at the digs ready for him. I sold the car, you see.'

'Thank you, sir. That's quite clear, I think. And what did you do with yourself last night?'

'Last night? Oh, I see.' His breath came out in a long sigh. 'Well, I'm all right there. I was at Valerie's birthday party and we kept it up rather. I didn't get home till nearly two. But we had keys — the landlady's very accommodating — so we let ourselves in and disturbed nobody.'

'We?'

'Yes, self and Bill McBride, who shares my digs.'

Spratt nodded sideways at Howard. 'Check with the lady, if she's still outside, just for the record, will you?'

Crayston glared at Howard's departing back. 'Look, I can bring you a dozen witnesses to prove I was at the party. And that I never left it. Don't you believe me?'

Spratt grinned. 'I'm a policeman. Which is the same as admitting I've got a nasty suspicious mind.'

Howard returned with an 'Okay, sergeant,' and Spratt told Crayston that would be all, and thanks.

They went back to the administration office. Mrs. Hopkins, with more lists in front of her, was awaiting them.

'I've dug out a Malcolm for you, the only one we have here,' she said. 'Malcolm South, first year.'

'Could you describe his appearance?'

'Small — only just over five feet, I'd say — very fair hair, soft, like a girl's, a pathetic attempt at a beard and a simply terrible stammer.'

Spratt shook his head. 'Not our man. Couldn't you possibly dig up a Malcolm, fairly tall, dark-haired?'

'Sorry!'

Howard spoke diffidently. 'It definitely was a Christian name, was it, sergeant? Couldn't have been a surname?'

Spratt frowned. 'I suppose it could have, come to think of it. You see,' he explained to Mrs. Hopkins, 'we're having to go on a reported conversation — what is it, lad?'

Howard was jogging his arm. The constable's eyes had been reading Mrs. Hopkins's list, upside down, as it lay on the table before her.

'How about that one, sergeant?'

Spratt stepped behind Mrs. Hopkins to follow Howard's pointing finger. It was resting on a name — Markham.

'Ah,' he said. 'Could be. Could be, at that.'

'Brian Markham. He's a local boy and he fits your description,' Mrs. Hopkins said. 'Address, 14 Hilltop Road. Wait a minute, now. Time-tables . . . Yes. He has a free afternoon today. You may find him at home.'

Spratt thanked her again and they went back to Penn Road, where Spratt had left his car. The policeman was no longer on duty outside Number Two.

'We'll get back to H.Q.,' the sergeant said. 'I don't know about you, lad, but my next bit of investigation'll be on some canteen sausages!'

4

The after-lunch conference took place in Hallam's office. The Chief Inspector sat at his desk, Spratt had his own small table near the window and Howard, bidden to attend, was seated in the background.

'Dr. Ransome has got a move on,' Hallam began, lifting a typed report from a folder, 'and he's turned up a bit of a surprise for us. While he's established Bradley was killed sometime during the late evening of yesterday, he states the smoothing iron was not the only object which was used on him. He was first knocked out — and the blow could have been fatal — by something in the nature of a round-ended bar or stick. The iron was used later. He is quite convinced, by a depression in the skull bone, that this was so.'

'Which makes you think,' Spratt muttered.

Hallam nodded. 'Let's look at the

probable picture. Bradley went back to Penn Road sometime during the evening. He let himself in with his street-door key, unlocked the archives room, switched on the light and sat down at his desk. There was nothing in the way of paper or books on that desk to suggest he'd returned to clear up some work, and it's not at all likely he'd have gone back for that purpose, anyway. We can take it he was there to meet somebody.'

'Humpkin. Half-past nine,' Spratt put in. 'Though that's a queer time for an appointment, say what you like.'

'We've got to accept it as a theory, though,' Hallam argued. 'So we go on from there. Humpkin — or somebody else — arrives. Somebody armed with a club-type weapon. Bradley was killed without a struggle. The killer just stepped behind him and struck. Then, maybe to make a good job of it, or merely to confuse the issue, the said killer picked up the iron which Bradley had been using that day and smashed him up with it. Now, can this point to some sort of quarrel?'

'With Humpkin?' Spratt queried. 'Seems to me we'd better get hold of that fellow as soon as possible.'

'That mightn't prove so easy. I've put a couple of the clerks on to check telephone and street directories and electoral rolls. Up to now nothing has turned up. It doesn't look as if he's a local man. We'll have to plough on, further afield.'

Hallam put the medical report aside.

'Fingerprints. None at all on the iron, which had been very carefully wiped. Only Bradley's on his desk and chair. Others — all Bradley's — in various parts of the room. That line is absolutely dead.' He shrugged, and closed the folder. 'You saw this chap Crayston?'

'Yes.' Spratt gave a brief outline of the interview. 'I've no reason to think he wasn't telling the truth. If Crayston had killed Bradley to free himself from the debt, surely he would have searched Bradley's wallet and removed the paper? And as for the Malcolm Mrs. Atkinson heard mentioned, here's the story about that.'

Hallam listened, then turned to Howard. 'Nice work, Howard, spotting the surname.' He leaned forward. 'We haven't seen Dr. Peel yet, of course. That row he had with Bradley is probably all over and done with, but maybe, for the record . . . Yes, we'll fit it in when he returns. At the moment, the job is to interview Markham. Take Howard with you, sergeant.' He gestured at his In tray. 'I've a load of stuff here which won't wait any longer and meanwhile we'll hope something turns up on friend Humpkin.'

Hilltop Road, where Brian Markham lived, was part of a residential area on the east side of the city. Spratt swung the car into the kerbside opposite Number Fourteen. There was a small, untidy plot of garden in front of the house and a powerful, though aged, motor-cycle was jacked up on the cracked concrete path. Spratt's ring at the front door brought a small, faded woman with greying hair. She wore a flowered apron over a dark dress and she looked at them with the guarded, half-aggressive air of a housewife whose life is eternally plagued by doorstep salesmen.

'Yes, what is it?'

Smoothly, Spratt produced his warrant card. 'Police, madam. C.I.D. You are Mrs. Markham?'

'That's me.' There was a flicker of apprehension in her eyes. 'What you want, then?'

'Just a word with Mr. Brian Markham. Is he at home?'

'Our Brian? He's upstairs, studying. In his room. What you want him for?'

'We're making some inquiries and we think he can help us, Mrs. Markham. Would you let him know we're here?'

The woman hesitated, and then, 'Perhaps you'd better come in.' She stood aside to usher them into a small crowded front room. 'I haven't had time to do in here yet today.' She didn't ask them to sit down. 'I'll tell him.'

They heard her dragging slowly upstairs, then her voice, and a man's answering it, in a room above. Hurried footsteps descended and a young man came into the room. He had a narrow, long-jawed face. He wore a high-necked blue sweater, jeans and scuffed suede shoes. His hair colouring and build fitted the description given by Mrs. Atkinson.

'I'm Brian Markham,' he said. 'Me mum says you want to see me.'

Spratt smiled genially. 'Sorry to interrupt your work, Mr. Markham. We shouldn't keep you long. Just a few questions — in private, I think.'

The youth swung round and spoke to his mother, who was hovering in the doorway.

'Get lost, mum.' He stepped to the door and began to close it. 'And no listening outside, either,' he said roughly as he banged the door shut. 'Now, then, mister, let's have it.'

'We're making some inquiries into the death of Mr. Edmund Bradley.' Spratt made the statement flatly and paused, his eyes on Markham's face.

'Bradley,' Markham repeated, and then his fists clenched at his sides. 'Hell! You don't mean the old boy in Reg. Hist., do you? The archivist bloke?'

'Yes, sir. He was killed last night in his room at the university. A case of homicide, sir.'

'You don't say?' Both Spratt and Howard received the impression, at that moment, that young Markham was suddenly thinking very hard. 'Er — bad luck,' he commented lamely, and added, 'But I don't see why you should have to come here about it.'

'You knew Mr. Bradley quite well, I believe?'

'Me? I knew him, naturally. I've been in to borrow books from his library. So have dozens of others.'

'I understood you visited his flat, about a month ago.'

'Me? Visited his flat?' He moved restlessly. 'That's a bloody lie, whoever said it.'

'We have a witness who heard a quarrel taking place in Mr. Bradley's flat. Mr. Bradley addressed the other man as Markham. The witness saw this visitor leave the premises.'

Markham stepped to the door, opened it and looked into the passage outside. He closed the door, apparently satisfied, and perched himself on the edge of a sagging, old-fashioned sofa.

'Look, mister, I'll come clean. I was there, we did have a bit of a row and maybe I did sort of threaten him. But it was all in fun, like, all over nothing.'

'You'd better give us some details, I think.'

'Well . . . Mr. Bradley got very tough about overdue books. If you kept them out too long you could bet on a rocketing from him. Well, there was this book, you see. I'd taken it out and it got misplaced. So Bradley got on to my back about it. I kept promising to return it, hoping it would turn up — I looked all over — and he got nasty about it. Said if it wasn't in by a certain date he'd report it, and I'd have to pay for it. Expensive book, too, cost several quid. Well, just as I'd given up all hope, blow me if I didn't come across it, underneath a pile of papers upstairs here, where I'd never thought of looking. I thought, right, I'll put the old boys' mind at rest. I wanted to give the bike a bit of a run anyway, so I rode over to his place and delivered this book.'

'You were familiar with Mr. Bradley's private address, then?'

He answered that one confidently enough.

'Sure. He was a keen photographer, specialized in historical stuff, and he asked a few of us over, just before the long vac last year, to a sherry party and to see some slides he'd recently made.'

Spratt pressed on. 'What was the title of this book you borrowed and kept for so long?'

'Um . . . Something about parish registers. Yes, that's it — *Studying Local History from Parish Registers*. Crummiest book you ever read.'

'There's a file of library loan cards in Mr. Bradley's room, sergeant,' Howard said. 'That book will be recorded on one of them under Mr. Markham's name, and marked overdue. Easy to check.'

'Yes,' Spratt said, and grinned suddenly. 'And check it we shall. Now you tell me, sir, why it was necessary to have a row with Mr. Bradley merely because you returned a book to him.'

'Well, you see . . . It was my fault, really. I'm a bit short on the temper, I admit it — you should ask my mum

— and when the old boy began to give me a ticking off for not looking after his blasted book — well, I'm not a schoolkid any longer, and I just wasn't going to wear it from him. So I told him — oh, to keep his trap shut, or something like that, and it narked him and he threatened to report me to Prof. Kirk for insolence. That made me real mad and I yelled at him — something, I dunno what it was now. He told me to cool down and I did. I apologized and that was that. We parted the best of pals. Oh, and I've just remembered something else. It's quite likely you won't find anything in the library to say I borrowed that book, because Bradley mentioned to me he'd forgotten to record it.' He shrugged his shoulders and laughed, a dry, rasping sound. 'Proves the best of us can slip up, doesn't it?'

'Yes,' Spratt said. He stood up, taking his time over it. 'Now, then, young man. Let's stop playing silly beggars, shall we? You're in a very nasty spot. You are known to have quarrelled with Mr. Bradley, and you can tell us the proper story, either here or after we charge you at the station.'

'But I swear I've just — '

'Look,' Spratt cut in. 'Nearly every day of my life I have to listen to some fellow spinning a yarn which is as phony as hell. In time you get the sound of it, so you can't be mistaken. Well, what's it to be? Here? Or there?'

Markham stumbled to his feet. 'You're just trying to trap a confession out of me.' His face flamed and his hands balled into fists. 'That's it, isn't it?' He was shouting now. 'And you won't leave me alone till you've got it out of me. You wouldn't be here if Bradley hadn't said something — after all he promised, too!'

Spratt took a step forward, seized him by the upper arms and forced him back on to the sofa.

'Take a pull on yourself, you young fool!' he growled. 'And control that temper of yours. You don't want your mother in here, do you? You don't want her to know what a crass idiot you've been?'

Markham collapsed suddenly, like an

emptied bag. He put his head between his hands, elbows on his knees.

'All right,' he said. 'I give in. I've sense enough to know, in a job like this . . . Okay, then. Bradley had something on me. He told me to see him at his flat, to get it straightened out there. Away from the university, like.

'Look. I went into Reg. Hist. early one morning. Just after nine. I had to leave an essay for Clift. I was just inside the door when I saw these two keys lying in a corner by the stairs. I picked them up and pocketed them. Impulse, like. I knew they weren't the secretary's because when I got upstairs she was just opening her office. They couldn't have been Prof. Kirk's because he was away at the time. Clift keeps his keys on a chain, I've seen it. I guessed maybe the cleaners had dropped them.

'Well, I just shoved them into my pocket, like I said. I thought they could be useful. Mr. Clift was due to set us an important grading test and it struck me I might get a chance of a preliminary look at the papers. I needed it. So one evening, when they'd all gone, I slipped into the house and opened the door of Clift's room. No luck with the papers. I couldn't resist forcing the flimsy drawers of his desk. They just asked for it. I found money. It seemed silly to leave it there. And there was a smashing camera, too.'

He writhed under Spratt's unequivocal gaze.

'All right, all right! It was a damn silly thing to do. Next day I had a message to see Mr. Bradley. I went to his room. He said he wanted to have a talk with me, at his flat that night, where we'd be private and no interruptions. He said I'd better turn up if I knew what was good for me. He'd seen me coming out of Number Two that evening. Seems he'd been using that mounting iron of his and had left it out on the table. Couldn't remember if he'd switched it off. He was scared of a fire starting and had come back to check on it.

'So I went to his place. He accused me of taking the camera and the dough. Said he'd kept quiet about it because he didn't want to spoil my career. I tried to bluff it out, but he had it on me, I knew. Made me promise to return the stuff and said I could do so anonymously, like. If I did, he'd say nothing. I hadn't spent any of the money. I took everything back, including the keys, and left them outside Mr. Clift's door. And that's God's truth.'

'I hope it is,' Spratt said. 'And you can come down to the station tomorrow and put it all in writing. Don't worry, it'll be kept private unless . . . Where were you last night? And let's have a bit more truth.'

'Down at Price's garage. I often spend time there. Pick up a bit on the side, doing jobs for Taff Price.'

'That's the place in Willow Street?'

Markham nodded. 'I got down there about seven. There were several rush jobs in. We worked on till just after half-past ten. I got home here about eleven, as mum'll tell you. She waited up for me. I had supper, went to bed.'

He was looking at Spratt appealingly now, a very frightened young man indeed.

'We'll check it, of course. We'll check it thoroughly. So Evan Price is a friend of yours? Well, well!'

'Look, I just help out at his garage. No harm in that, is there? It was through this chap at the university, you see. Gerry Dickson. He got to know I'm a bit of a mechanic, and he works there too in his spare time. So he got me in.'

'Right,' Spratt said. 'We'll be on our way. You've no telephone here, have you?'

'No. Can't afford luxuries like that.'

'Take a tip, then. Don't go dashing out to the box down the road to call up Price's and ask them to fix any alibis for you. You'll be watched, you see.'

'Which,' he commented to Howard as they returned to their car, 'is a case of telling a lie to further the course of justice. Not that I think he'll have any need for alibi-fixing, do you?'

'No. You scared the truth out of him, sarge. And he did return the stuff he'd pinched. Bradley, obviously, didn't intend to take further action on that, so there seems no point in Markham killing him.'

Spratt backed the car into a driveway, swung it round and headed back for the city. 'All the same, we'll check on him. I'll drop you in Granby Street and you can get a bus across to Willow Street. Do you know Price's joint?'

'Can't say I do.'

'You'll find it easy enough. Only, watch your step, lad. Taff Price is a slippery customer. Hard to lay your hands on him.'

He was silent for a while, negotiating the traffic of the main road into which he had turned.

'Motive,' he said, 'that's the trouble in this case. Who would want to bash an inoffensive fellow like Bradley? 'Find the motive, and you'll find your man.' Sounds easy, doesn't it? Ah, well, we'll get there in the end, I expect. We usually do.'

5

Howard halted at one end of Willow Street and gave it a quick looking-over. This was a part of the city to which neither duty nor pleasure had hitherto brought him. He didn't think much of it.

Willow Street was bordered, along one of its sides, by a dingy brick wall, topped by jagged glass set in concrete, behind which ran a railway line. On the other side of the street a cluster of small shops crowded at each end; between them were warehouses, a public house, and, separating this from Price's garage, a derelict, broken-windowed factory. The garage, with its bright red petrol pumps, its garishly-lettered advertising signs, stood out like an overblown poppy in a patch of faded weeds.

Howard walked slowly towards it, not at all too sure of himself. This was the first really responsible job which had fallen to his lot as a detective constable and he was wondering just how to handle it. Had Evan Price, the garage owner, been an ordinary, law-abiding citizen, entirely clean of police suspicion, Howard would have had no worries. Walk in, introduce himself, produce his credentials if asked for them, and get cracking. But Jack Spratt had hinted that the Price set-up was far from innocent, in which case the faintest smell of a policeman on the premises would be likely to close everybody up like a clam.

He glanced at his watch. Ten to four — he'd better get a move on. All right, then. Play it casual to start with.

He strolled quietly up to the garage. It lay back from the street, with a forecourt just wide enough to take a car alongside the pumps.

He walked in. Electric lights from the roof — for the garage workshop windows were thick with grime — cast hard shadows on a filthy concrete floor. Somewhere a hammer was tapping gently and a transistor set was tunelessly grinding out the latest pop hit. There were six or eight cars standing about but

Howard could see nobody working on those near him. A small office on the left of the double doors was also empty.

He waited impatiently for almost a minute and was about to go in search of one of the hidden mechanics when something stirred beneath one of the cars on his right. Looking closer, he saw a pair of feet, the legs of stained overalls and one end of a wheeled crawler trolley. He was considering whether to address the workman beneath the car when a door opened at the rear of the garage and a short, thickset man with crinkly black hair and a lean, blue-chinned face came quickly towards him.

'Good afternoon, sir. Wanting me, is it?' The greeting and the interrogation rang musically with the accent of Wales.

Howard had decided on the play of his hand.

'Brian Markham about?' he asked.

'Brian Markham. Well, look, he isn't usually here at this time of day. He's a stu-dent, at the university. You go there, boy, if you want him.'

'Oh, it doesn't really matter. I know he

comes here to give you a hand now and then, and I just wondered . . . But that'll be evenings and week-ends, I suppose?'

'And in his 'olidays, too, indeed. Good mechanic, he is. A waste of time for him at that old university. Well, that's it, boy. He isn't here.'

Howard shrugged his shoulders as if it didn't matter. He half-turned away, then swung back.

'Was he here last night? You see, there was this dance, and he didn't turn up.'

He saw the quick tensioning of Price's black brows and, in dismay, he knew he had overplayed that hand of his. He had snapped the question out in too much of a policeman-like manner and the impromptu explanation which followed it had been far too hesitating, far too unconvincing. Price stood there, looking at him very keenly.

The crawler trolley was propelled from beneath the nearby car with a shrill squeaking which set Howard's teeth on edge. A young man swung himself up into a sitting position. He had fiery red hair, worn long, an ill-nourished red beard and

75

streaks of oily grease all over his face. His mouth twisted as he grinned at Howard.

'I'm a pal of Brian Markham's, comrade. But I don't know you. You at the university, too?'

Howard returned his gaze levelly. 'I'm not.'

'And that's a pity.' He spoke with a slight local accent. 'An intelligent-looking young feller like you's the type we want there.' He raised his voice. 'Oh, Sid! Here a minute!'

Price said suddenly, 'Don't you be a fool, now, Red. And the cus-tom-er, he wants that Vanguard finished for tonight. Promised him, I did.'

The other tilted his chin and looked at him cheekily.

'You go and get lost now, Taff, bach. I'll have this load of junk ready in time.'

Price spat into a pool of oil at his feet and turned away, walking out through the entrance doors. A young mechanic, with an ape-like face sauntered up, carrying a two-foot long spanner. 'I 'ear you calling me, Red.' He cackled foolishly.

'I need your valued assistance for just

one moment, Sid. Only, be careful of that spanner. If you were to drop it on this gentleman's toes, now, you might lame him for life, Sid, mightn't you?'

The empty laugh came again. 'You mean — like so?'

Howard had sensed trouble. It was time he came out into the open. His hand went to his wallet.

'Look here — '

He saw the flash of the falling spanner, thrown, not dropped, deliberately aimed at his feet. Quickly, he stepped sideways.

The youth they had called Red thrust out a leg, tripping the detective neatly. He staggered, clutching at the bonnet of the car. But his fingers found no hold and he went down, arms and legs threshing, sprawling on his back on the grease-scummed floor.

'Oh, dear, dear!' Red sprang up in mock alarm and concern. 'Give a hand here, Sid, you clumsy clot.' And before Howard could gain control of his limbs he was hauled upright, with two oily hands solicitously wiping down the front of his jacket.

He jerked himself free and sprang back. He was furious, eyes blazing and fists clenched. He came lunging forward, and the sneering lips amid their thin fringe of beard tightened. Red spoke sharply.

'Hold it, copper! Very bad it would look in a report, wouldn't it?'

Howard forced himself back on his heels. The incisive words bit into his consciousness. He remembered what he was and where he was, and that policemen do not use physical force except in self-defence. But words — they were different.

'You rotten couple of louts! I — I'll — '
A fresh wave of fury choked him.

'Now, now, be reasonable.' Red put on a man-to-man tone. 'You know damn well it was a pure accident. Sid let the spanner slip out of his hand — '

'You practically told him — '

'Now you're imagining things. And the fact that you happened to trip over me was something I couldn't avoid. What say we forget it, eh? After Sid has apologized, of course.'

Sid stuck out a filthy hand.

'Sorry, mate. I'll be more careful next time.' He let the hand fall to his side when Howard pointedly ignored it. 'Hey, Red, didn't you call him copper?'

'A slip of the tongue, my dear Sid. I meant policeman, of course. You are, aren't you, comrade?'

'Yes.' Howard was realizing now, very bitterly, that he should have announced himself at once, and chanced it. 'You seem to know it all. What's your name?'

The other bowed mockingly. 'At your service — Gerald Dickson. Address, Monkbridge House, Wellingborough Road, Occupation, student, Deniston University. An earnest seeker after truth in the Faculty of Science, Department of Physics. And, to assuage your curiosity, I saw you going into the murder house in Penn Road this morning. Got your man yet?'

Howard ignored the query. He said, with as much dignity as he could muster, 'We are making inquiries with regard to people who used that building. Brian Markham is one of them. We've seen him and he has made a statement. He said he was here last night until this place closed at ten or thereabouts. It's my job to check that.'

Dickson stared wide-eyed at him. 'Whyever didn't you say so, when you came in, instead of all that fancy stuff about being a pal of his? Might have saved yourself a lot of trouble.' Sid turned away, concealing a grin. 'Right. Well, he was here all evening. I can swear to that. Evan Price will back me up, too.'

'No doubt he will,' Howard said acidly.

'You mean — just a minute, now. Yes.' Dickson pushed himself away from the car against which he had been leaning. 'If you would be good enough to accompany me, officer, I think I can give you the proof you need.'

Glumly, Howard followed him across to the small office by the entrance doors. Dickson went inside and began to rummage among the untidy heaps of papers which littered the top of a small desk.

'Here we are!' he said, and handed Howard an empty envelope. It was typewritten and addressed to Brian

Markham at his home. Howard turned it over. The back bore a sketch of a motor-car gear-box, done in bold, confident pencil strokes.

'All his own work!' Dickson's grin was back again. 'And, as you will have already noticed, done here last night.'

Howard managed to stop himself putting the obvious question, the question Dickson was aching to hear. He'd be damned, Howard told himself, if he'd ask this clot how the envelope proved . . . His brain clicked, and he turned the envelope over again.

'Yes,' he said. 'Postmarked the day before yesterday. From Manchester, so it would be delivered to Markham yesterday morning. And you can swear the drawing was done here last night?'

He had spiked Dickson's guns, but the physics student could not resist elaboration.

'The point is, you see, that Brian couldn't have been in possession of that envelope before yesterday morning. He had lectures all morning and a tutorial in the afternoon. Check that if you like. So he couldn't have arrived here till evening, which is what he did and used the envelope for the sketch then.'

Howard put the envelope into his pocket and was walking away when the garage owner came in again.

'You still here, then?' he asked.

Dickson spoke up. 'He's a C.I.D. bloke, Evan. Checking on Brian, wanting to know if he was here last night.'

'He was here all right. So you're C.I.D., are you? There's nice, now. A new boy you'll be. I haven't seen you before.'

'That's your misfortune.' The crack didn't come out as crisply as Howard had intended. 'Right, I'll be off.'

'Now wait a minute. Look, I don't like the police, or any-body else, coming into my premises on false pretences. You should have said who you was, straight off. Then we could have helped you proper.'

'All right, all right!' Howard knew he was being deliberately needled. He swung round and strode out of the garage, furious with the lot of them!

He stalked, stiff-legged, along the street

towards the bus-stop, helplessly raging. A nice mess he'd made of that job, trying to be clever. Here he was, with his suit practically ruined and a trio of jeering clots as witnesses to his confusion, all in the course of carrying out a simple inquiry.

He reached Albert Road, which ran parallel to Willow Street. Albert Road was lined by small grimy houses, their frontages on one side broken by an area of waste ground belonging to the Deniston Corporation. It was scheduled for a children's playground, to be elaborately fitted with all the latest amusements — some day. Meanwhile, the local juniors made the best use they could of it. It was muddy in wet weather and dusty in dry, but it was somewhere to go off the streets. There was a telephone box on the edge of the unbuilt area and Howard turned towards it, feeling for coppers.

His call was put through to Sergeant Spratt. 'I was wondering what had happened to you, young man,' Spratt said sharply. 'You've been long enough ringing in, haven't you? Did you strike trouble or something?'

'No, sarge, it's all right. I mean, I've established Markham spent the entire evening at Price's garage, as he said. In fact, I've documentary proof to back his story up.'

'Good. Well, you can get off home now. If you're needed again today we'll ring you there . . . Are you still listening?'

'I — Oh, sorry sarge. Something just took my attention. Yes, I heard what you said. I'll stay at home on call.'

He cradled the instrument but did not leave the box. While he had been telephoning, a car had come along the street, an old-time Ford Popular, and had been driven on to the waste ground in defiance of the No Parking notice prominently displayed there. It wasn't the offence which interested Howard, but he had noticed that the rear wall of Price's garage in Willow Street backed on to the empty space, and the man who had got out of the car was walking slowly in that direction. He was a well-made fellow, in his early thirties, Howard judged, with dark hair, and handsome, too, from the brief glimpse the detective had of him. As the man walked, he glanced at his wrist-watch. He went almost up to a small wooden door in the brick wall at the rear of the garage, hung about there for a minute or so and then came sauntering back towards his car. Howard picked up the telephone directory from its shelf and began to turn its leaves. The exercise gave him a chance to keep his head bent.

The door in the wall opened and the red-haired Dickson came out. He hurried across to the other man and began to talk quickly to him, pouring out a flood of words which the car-driver tried to halt with an upraised hand. Howard glimpsed the student's face. It was set and angry. Master Dickson didn't seem so pleased with himself now.

At that point Howard ducked out of the box and retreated behind the corner of the end house. He was curious, he would have given much to know who the man was and what business Dickson had with him. But he himself had no call to interfere; he certainly wasn't going to make a further fool of himself. He might as well go home, on the bus which was, at that moment, slowing at a stop on the opposite side of the street. Howard sprinted across and climbed aboard.

And then he had his first piece of luck that afternoon. The bus driver cut his engine, left his cab and went into a small confectioner's shop opposite the bus stop. A full minute and a half elapsed before he came out again, clutching a filled paper bag and throwing back some witticism over his shoulders at the unseen shop-owner.

Howard had used those ninety seconds to the full. From his upstairs seat, on the off side of the bus, he had a clear view of the Popular and the two who stood by it. He was willing to bet all his chances of future promotion that they were having an argument, an acrimonious one at that. Furthermore, to Howard's satisfaction, Dickson seemed to be on the losing end of it. As he craned his head back over his shoulder, when the bus moved slowly on, he caught a final glimpse of Dickson jerking himself away from the other man and hurrying back towards the garage.

Might be something, might be nothing, Howard ruminated. Clearly, the Popular owner had had an assignation with Dickson, but why there? Why not at the garage itself?

At the next stop a woman came upstairs and sat by Detective Constable Howard. She sniffed loudly several times and, at the first opportunity, changed her seat. Howard didn't blame her, his oily suit stank to heaven in his own nostrils.

But he had the number of the Ford Popular safely noted, and a very fair description of its driver.

6

Hallam scribbled his initials at the foot of a six-page report and pitched it at his overflowing Out tray. With a sigh of relief he reached for his tobacco pouch and pipe.

'That's the lot, thank Pete,' he muttered to Spratt. He flexed the fingers of his right hand. 'Talk about writers' cramp! Well, now.'

Spratt tapped a sheet of paper. 'Lab report on Bradley's clothes, etc. Completely and absolutely negative. Howard has checked Markham's story at Price's garage and seems satisfied with it.'

Hallam put a match to his pipe.

'D'you think that wily Welshman could have done a bit of wool-pulling?'

'I doubt it. Howard's raw yet, of course, but he has his head screwed on all right. Anyway, about Markham. That looks like another blank wall. Bradley had done Markham a good turn in keeping quiet about the theft of the money and the camera. Why should Markham kill him?'

'Oh, I agree, Jack.' Hallam sighed again. 'But we're getting nowhere. And I've had the A.C.C. on the line.'

'Urging rapid action, I'll bet, sir.' Spratt knew the methods of Daly, the Assistant Chief Constable.

'More than that. The university Vice-Chancellor had been on to him. Supremely important to have the case cleared up as soon as possible. As if we didn't know.'

His words were punctuated by a knock on the door. A duty sergeant entered smartly.

'A call from Northwood Station, sir,' he said. 'They relayed it on in case it had anything to do with this university job.'

'Carry on, White.'

'They had a message from a Mrs. Peel, sir.' White glanced at a pad in his hand. 'Ashlea, Churchill Road, Northwood. Her husband's on the staff at the university. He went to London yesterday afternoon. Told her he'd be staying at a friend's flat in Fulham, and would ring her when he arrived. He didn't, and apparently she became rather worried and rang this friend about an hour ago. Friend knew nothing about the husband. He hadn't turned up, wasn't expected, even. She felt she ought to do something about all this and rang the local station.'

'Thanks, White. Let Northwood know we're dealing with it, will you?' Hallam waited until the sergeant had gone, then he looked across at Spratt.

'Dr. Peel, of the Science Faculty,' he commented. 'The metallurgist who'd had a small war with Bradley. I think we'd better see the lady.'

'According to Professor Kirk, that trouble was all over and done with, sir.'

'Nevertheless, and even if only to satisfy the A.C.C., Jack, we'd better make the effort.'

Twenty minutes later they were heading northwards from the city. At the wheel, Spratt cut off, at last, along a secondary road which served a suburb of glaringly-new houses and shops.

'Another bit of good countryside gone for ever,' he commented sourly. 'When I was a lad we used to come out here for the day. It was all unspoilt then.'

'That's progress, Jack. Turn right at the crossroads ahead.' Hallam was navigating with the aid of a newly-published street map. Spratt swung the car on to a road of recently-laid concrete.

Ashlea was at the far end, quite isolated from its nearest neighbour. Stone-built, it stood well back from the road, with a gravelled drive, a two-car garage and a raw, partly-made garden.

Spratt pulled the car on to the gravel through the open double gates. They got out and walked towards the front door.

It was opened before they reached it. A woman stepped out beneath the porch, a small person in her late twenties, at the sight of whom the adjective 'fluffy' sprang to Hallam's mind. She had very fair, very fine hair, some strands of which had escaped from their setting. Her face was round, kittenish, and her eyes were large and blue. She wore a loose flowered dress, a necklace of amber beads, and bracelets jingled on her wrists as her hands flew up to her small curved mouth.

'Oh! Are you bringing news of my husband?'

'We are police officers, madam.' Hallam gave her their names. 'Your telephone call to the Northwood Police Station was handed on to us. We'd like a word with you, though we can't tell you anything about Dr. Peel yet.'

'Oh! Do you think he's had an accident, or even . . . You see, he promised to ring me and he never misses doing so when he's away, but he did this time so I rang up Charles in London and he didn't know a thing!'

'Let's go inside, shall we?' Hallam suggested. 'And I wouldn't start worrying yet, Mrs. Peel. You just tell us all the circumstances and I'm sure we'll be able to help.'

She gave a half-choked sob, but turned quickly and led them into a lounge, a large room, expensively furnished. She offered them chairs before she seated herself on a low stool beside the electric fire. She clasped her plump little hands round her knees and stared anxiously at her visitors.

'I do hope nothing has happened. Oh, I know it's quite foolish to worry, but, you see, it's so unlike Lewis — that's my husband, of course.'

'Let's start at the beginning,' Hallam said gently. 'Dr. Peel went to London yesterday afternoon. By car? Or train?'

'By train. He left on the two-forty. But he didn't know when he'd be back, exactly, which was rather odd, really, because . . . Well, it was all rather odd, in fact, and that's what is so worrying.'

'What was the object of the London visit?'

The knuckles of the clasped hands whitened. 'Some sort of scientific conference — at least, that's what he said, though he told me to call the university this morning and tell them he was away on private business. But the conference wasn't down in his book — his engagements book, you know. He keeps it on his desk in the study.' She unlinked her hands to gesture towards the ceiling. 'You see, I looked, after he had gone. And there wasn't any note of it. Besides, he always tells me beforehand when he has a conference coming up. These things are arranged in advance — well, they have to be, haven't they?'

'So Dr. Peel decided to go to London . . . ?'

'After he'd had this telephone message.'

'Telephone message,' Hallam repeated. 'Tell us about that.'

'Well.' Her hands went together again. 'It was just after we'd finished lunch. Lewis hadn't to go to the university yesterday afternoon but he'd brought some work home. He'd gone up to the study when the phone rang and I answered it. I said who I was and the caller — a man — said he must speak to Dr. Peel personally. So I ran upstairs and told Lewis and he came down and . . . Well, I pretended to go into the kitchen, but actually I stood by the kitchen door and listened.'

'Yes?'

'Lewis said, 'Peel here. What is it?' and then, 'Good God, no!' and a bit later, 'I'll come at once — be with you this evening.' He banged the phone down and called me. His face was white and I thought he looked as if he'd had a shock. I said, 'What on earth's happened?' and he smiled and said everything was all right but he'd have to leave at once. 'That scientific conference in Town, you know,' he said. 'I'd forgotten it was on tomorrow. Completely slipped my memory.'

'I asked him what conference, because it was the first I'd heard about it. And he said, oh, it was a very hush-hush thing which he wasn't supposed to talk about, even to me. Well, I know he does work for the government so I thought . . . Anyway, he had to rush to get ready. I helped him to pack and drove him to the station to catch the train. The last thing he said, as the train was moving out, was that he'd ring me. But he hasn't done, you see.'

Hallam had been listening attentively. 'You've no idea who your husband's caller was?' he asked.

'No. You see, he didn't give his name.'

'Are you aware of the tragedy which has taken place at the university, Mrs. Peel?'

'Oh, yes!' She gestured towards a copy

of the evening paper which had been thrown down on a table. 'I was just reading about it when you arrived. Isn't it terrible? My husband knew Mr. Bradley. In fact, he wrote an article against Lewis. Lewis was very annoyed at the time, I remember.'

'Tell me, has your husband ever had to rush off like this before?'

'Never.' The worry was back on her pretty face again. 'And him forgetting this conference — I mean, he has a secretary at the university, a Mrs. Brill. She's quite marvellous, he always says. She'd never fail to remind him about a thing like that.'

Hallam sat forward in his chair. 'Now, look here. Suppose you ring your husband's London friend again, Mrs. Peel. Do it now, will you? He may have news for you.'

'But Charles promised to ring back . . . All right, I will.' She sprang up as if she were relieved at having something definite to do. 'Excuse me, please,' she added from the door.

Hallam and Spratt exchanged glances as the door closed.

'Well, Jack?'

'One or two odd points, sir. Whether they tie up with our job I wouldn't like to say. She's fair bothered, isn't she?'

'She is.' Hallam rose and walked to the fireplace. He was standing there, examining an example of very neo-modern art when Mrs. Peel returned. She looked completely downcast.

'No news at all, I'm afraid, Chief Inspector.'

'There's plenty of time for that yet,' Hallam assured her. 'Your husband's secretary — has she a private telephone number?'

'Yes, she's on the phone, but I don't know her number. She lives — let me see, we went to tea there once — Park Road, or Park Crescent or it could be Park View. It isn't Park Street, I do know that.'

'I think it would be as well to give her a ring. Sergeant Spratt will do that, if he may.'

'Of course. The directory's by the phone in the hall. Mrs. Brill. Park something.'

'I'll find it, madam.' Spratt went out.

He came back to find Hallam and Mrs. Peel discussing the pros and cons of central heating.

'Park Crescent is the address, madam. I spoke to Mrs. Brill. She has no knowledge of any London engagements Dr. Peel had. She received your message this morning, saying he wouldn't be in, further than that she knows nothing.'

'Lewis asked me to let them know he'd be away for a few days,' Mrs. Peel told them again. 'Which I did, though I didn't speak to Mrs. Brill herself. I — '

The telephone in the hall began to ring. Mrs. Peel leapt up.

'That'll be Charles Mitchell ringing me back, or perhaps it's Lewis himself!' She ran from the room, leaving the door open. They heard her voice, breathless with eagerness. 'Yes? This is Hazel Peel,' and then, after a brief interval, tones of flat, weary disappointment. 'Very well, I'll tell him. Hold on, please.'

She came back slowly. 'It's for you, Chief Inspector.'

'Thank you.' Hallam moved towards the door. 'I took the liberty of asking our people to ring your number if I should be wanted.' He went out to the hall.

'Hallam here . . . What? . . . When? . . . Right, I'll meet you there in a quarter of an hour. Twenty minutes at most.' Hallam stepped to the door of the lounge.

'We have to get back, Mrs. Peel. Now, try not to worry, and if your husband, or his friend, rings with news, let the Northwood Police Station know. We'll do all we can to help.'

The evening was overcast and it was becoming rapidly dark now. They returned to the car. Spratt switched on his lights.

'Well, sir, what's new?'

'It's back to the university for us, Jack. Somebody's just discovered that a safe in Peel's office has been broken into, and some very important papers have disappeared from it!'

7

'It appears,' Hallam said when Spratt had made the turn back on to the main road, 'that one of the lecturers in the Department of Metallurgy had occasion to go to a safe in Dr. Peel's office this evening. The safe should have been closed and locked, of course. It wasn't — the door was partly ajar. The chap pulled it open and found the safe cleared out, completely. He rang the head porter at once — our pal Carr, I gathered — and Carr reported it to the police. B Division got the call, naturally, and Inspector Bates went along. As it was obviously a C.I.D. job, well, that's how we got the word.'

The campus was brightly lit when they drove on to it through the handsome arch at the main entrance. From the Student's Union building a solid wave of noise ebbed and flowed — the flow was long and sustained, the ebb exceedingly brief — and behind uncurtained windows a packed mass of bodies swayed and gyrated to a shrieking, thudding band. As the detectives got out of their car they caught a glimpse, through another window, of the crowded Union bar, with three white-jacketed attendants struggling to supply the orders of a jostling mob of youths and girls.

The head porter's manner was much mellower this evening. He greeted them quite jocularly.

'Ah, gentlemen! So we've had to fetch you here again! Much more of this sort of thing and they'll be giving you honorary degrees, I shouldn't wonder. Now, then. You need to be at Metallurgy. Down the steps again, turn to your right past the Physics Block, and you're there. You'll see a board directing you. Dr. Peel's office is on the first floor, along the corridor on the left.'

They found a uniformed constable on duty outside Dr. Peel's office. He saluted smartly and held the door open for them.

Within, there was a large, comfortable room with wide windows, an expensive carpet and a handsome desk at which

Inspector Bates was lolling at ease, reading an evening paper, while a sergeant was examining, with a faint air of puzzlement, the titles of the books in one of the three large bookcases with which the office was equipped. Bates put down his paper. He was a big, bulky man, grey-haired, with a bear-like ponderousness of movement. But even at this late hour of the day he looked every inch the police-officer, his well-fitting uniform speckless and his buttons and rank badges sparkling under the office's strip lighting. He got to his feet.

'Ah, William. I thought you'd be in on this, after what happened here this morning.'

Hallam grinned. 'The Uniform Branch passing the buck as usual, eh, Tom? Well, we'll help you out once more.'

'That's big of you,' Bates replied gravely. Suddenly, his tones were crisp, incisive.

'The man you want to see is named Firth. He's a lecturer here, Dr. Peel's chief assistant. Unfortunately, he won't be available till nine-thirty.' He glanced at his watch. 'Half an hour yet. He's giving an evening lecture to a bunch of technicians from somewhere or other. Actually, it seems, Peel was booked to do this but he's been called away and Firth felt he ought to stand in, rather than have the lecture cancelled. Right.

'The safe's behind that door yonder.' He pointed. 'It's a sort of storeplace and the safe's at the far end of it. Tumbler lock, old-fashioned. Peel, Firth and a secretary, Mrs. Brill, were the only people who knew the combination. Firth went to it this evening to get some lecture notes from it. Found the door ajar and the safe cleaned out. I've been in touch with Mrs. Brill over the phone and she'll be along here as soon as she can. You'll know more about contacting Peel than I do.'

Hallam shook his head. 'At the moment, Dr. Peel seems to have vanished. His wife's quite out of touch with him — he should have turned up last night at an address in London, but he didn't.'

'So — ' Bates's heavy eyebrows rose.

'No reason yet to get unduly alarmed, I

think. At least, that's what I've told his wife. Well, let's have a look at the body.'

Sergeant Ballantyne stepped forward to open the door of what proved to be a large, cupboard-like place, fitted on each side with shelves, some of which held pieces of scientific apparatus. The safe was built into the rear of the small room. The safe door was open, its shelves completely bare. Bates spoke from the doorway.

'Fingerprints. I haven't done anything about that yet. There is the possibility, according to Firth, the lecturer, that the safe could have been left not properly closed. He doesn't think it at all likely, though it did happen once, some time back. Since then they've taken particular care.'

'Did he say what was in it?'

'He hummed and hawed a bit about that. He hadn't any stuff of his own in there, as it happened. They use it for very special private material — notes, drawings, such as that. Material it wouldn't be wise to leave around loose.'

Hallam came back into the office.

'What about this outer door? Was it kept locked?'

'I put that to Firth. There is a key, but nobody seems to have bothered with it. He thought Mrs. Brill might know where it was. That's her office, through there.' Bates pointed to a communicating door. 'We've had a look round it — her door on to the corridor is locked, but not that one — but there's nothing to help us there, on the surface, that is.'

The door opened and a young woman came into the room.

'I'm Mrs. Brill,' she said and smiled pleasantly. 'An Inspector Bates rang me . . . '

'Yes, madam.' Bates lumbered forward. 'Sorry to drag you away from home as late as this, but it was necessary.' He introduced Hallam and Spratt, and his own sergeant, Ballantyne. 'We're waiting for Mr. Firth to finish a lecture. Meanwhile, we'll see what you can tell us.'

Mrs. Brill peeled off her gloves. 'I'd like to see the safe first, Inspector.'

'Certainly.' He led the way to the store

cupboard. She was looking shaken when she came back into the main room and accepted Bates's invitation to sit at Dr. Peel's desk.

'Now, Mrs. Brill.' Bates pulled up a chair opposite her, but before he could put his first question a tall, thin, haggard-looking man came quickly in from the corridor. He had sparse, mousey hair, a prominent forehead and large red ears which stood out almost at right-angles to the sides of his head. An academic gown was over his arm, he carried a folder of papers in one hand. His manner was tense, highly-strung.

'I cut my lecture as short as I could,' he said to Bates. He seemed not to be aware of Hallam and Spratt, nor of Mrs. Brill. 'And believe you me, Inspector, that was the worst hour, I think, I ever spent. I was depending on using Dr. Peel's notes, you see. And as a result I badly mixed up my coefficients at one point and was corrected, in a loud voice, by one of my audience. Most shaming!' He laughed, in a high-pitched tremolo, and flinging the gown and the papers on to a side table, he took out a handkerchief and mopped at his high brow.

'Sit down, sir,' Bates said, solidly calm. 'Now, that's better. You know Mrs. Brill, of course.'

'Eileen!' He blinked his eyes at her. 'I didn't see you. What are you doing here?'

'Chief Inspector Hallam and Sergeant Spratt of the C.I.D.,' Bates ploughed on. 'Mr. Hallam is in charge of the case of the history archivist. Now, I know it'll be a boring job, telling your story again, Mr. Firth, but the chief inspector would like to hear it from your own lips.' He smiled at Mrs. Brill. 'Ladies second, for once? You don't mind?'

'Of course not.' Her answering smile was warm, intimate.

'Then off you go, Mr. Firth.'

The lecturer crossed his legs and leaned back.

'Mrs. Brill came to my room this morning — I'm next door to her along the corridor, just this side of the labs — and told me Dr. Peel had been called away suddenly to London. She was concerned about his lecture this evening, we talked the matter over and I decided to deputise for him. I needed, of course, his detailed formulae, various figures and calculations — his actual lecture notes, in fact. I was here in this room with him yesterday when he said he would put them in the safe. Quite naturally, I expected to find them there this evening. But the safe was open and empty. I was exceedingly agitated and alarmed, knowing what that safe should have contained. Beside the lecture notes and other papers, I mean.' He mopped at his face again and addressed Mrs. Brill.

'Eileen — do you think? — the confidential stuff, you know. Or should it not be mentioned?'

Mrs. Brill said quietly, 'These gentlemen are police, Mr. Firth. They must be told everything.'

'Of course, of course.' He swallowed, balling the handkerchief in one fist.

'Dr. Peel was working on a most important government project. It was to do with the problem of metal fatigue, particularly with reference to various new alloys. That is all I need reveal, except that his research had reached a final stage. You will realize this is all extremely top secret.'

Bates said, 'Of course, sir.'

'And that is why,' Firth went on, 'I felt it my duty to call the police, Inspector. Because Dr. Peel kept all the papers, the calculations, the formulae connected with this project, in the safe. I realized the implications of what I had found — or failed to find, to be precise.' Bates sat forward to put a question, but Firth stopped him with an upraised hand.

'You are about to ask, did it not occur to me that Dr. Peel might have taken this material away with him? Might it not now be safe in his own possession? But, you see, everything had gone from the safe — everything. As if a robbery had taken place.'

'Well, sir,' Bates replied, 'we have got to establish, if we can, whether Dr. Peel did, or did not, remove the important stuff.'

'He didn't,' Mrs. Brill answered. 'I mean, he didn't take it away with him when he left at lunchtime yesterday. He had a batch of students' test papers to correct at home. I packed them into his brief case, fastened it and handed it to him as he left. He was carrying nothing else.'

'Fair enough,' Bates said. 'Now, then. This is a combination-lock safe. You, Mr. Firth, knew the combination, you told me Dr. Peel and Mrs. Brill also knew it. And nobody else.'

'That is correct. Isn't it, Eileen?' Firth appealed.

'Perfectly correct, Inspector. And for extra security, the combination was changed every six months.'

'Right,' Bates said. 'And can we establish when the safe was opened, officially, last?'

'I put a file of confidential reports on our third year students — work reports — there on Friday last, four days ago,' Mrs. Brill replied. 'I haven't had occasion to go to the safe since. We didn't use it very often,' she added.

'Mr. Firth?'

'I haven't been near the thing for at least a fortnight, until this evening.'

'I see.' Bates paused to consider. 'So it

appears Dr. Peel used it last, when he put his notes away for the lecture this evening. Apart from them, and the project stuff, and the reports you mentioned, what else was in the safe, Mrs. Brill?'

'There was a folder with plans and details of a lab extension which is due to be started soon, quite a pile of correspondence Dr. Peel had had with various foreign scientists. There was also a collection of micro-photographs, in colour, of metals under stress. And various other odds and ends though nothing of extreme importance.'

Bates looked at Hallam. 'Anything to add, Chief Inspector?'

'I think not, at the moment. Mrs. Brill and Mr. Firth have been very helpful but I imagine they've taken us as far as they can.'

'So do I.' Bates stood up. 'We'll carry on here for a while. And we'll wish you good night and thank you for your assistance, both of you.'

'Oh, good!' Firth sprang up. 'It's my wife's birthday and we'd asked a few friends in. When this lecture thing turned up she said she'd hold the fort till I got back so if you don't mind . . . I suppose you've come in your own car, Eileen, so there's no need for me . . . ? Oh, good, good!'

He wished them all a flurried farewell and almost leapt through the doorway. Mrs. Brill was still seated and showed no signs of moving. She looked hard at Bates, then at Hallam. Finally, she turned to address Spratt.

'You rang me earlier this evening, sergeant, asking if I could account for Dr. Peel's sudden call to London. I couldn't, but I've been thinking about it since.'

'Yes, madam?'

'He certainly had no official conference on hand. I am aware of all his engagements, so he wasn't telling Mrs. Peel the truth there. Now, I should have remembered something else, when I was speaking to you, but it only struck me later. Whoever it was who called Dr. Peel at home tried to reach him at the university first. I feel sure of this.

'I was back at my office here yesterday after lunch. A call came for Dr. Peel. I said he was not in and could I take a message. The caller — it was a man — said he must speak to Dr. Peel personally and would I please give him Dr. Peel's private number. Naturally, I asked who was calling and was told to never mind that, to give the number quickly, the matter was urgent. I read out the number from the list by the phone.' Mrs. Brill raised her hands in self-deprecation. 'Am I just going on and on?'

'On the contrary,' Hallam said. 'It's all very interesting. I'm sure Inspector Bates agrees with me.'

'Er — yes.' Bates wasn't entirely sure he did. 'Well, that's about it, Mrs. Brill. Unless anything else occurs to you?'

She swung herself neatly to her feet, shaking her head.

'And what's it add up to?' Hallam asked when Sergeant Ballantyne had closed the door behind Mrs. Brill.

'In my reckoning, to a C.I.D. job,' Bates returned promptly. 'So it's over to you, Bill. And I devoutly hope, for your sake, that Peel hasn't done a Burgess and Maclean, taking his stuff over with him, despite what the secretary said.'

He gestured to his sergeant. 'Let's be off, Jim. Oh, and we'll take our chap outside with us. Okay by you, Bill?'

Hallam nodded and wished them good night. Spratt's hand hovered over the desk telephone.

'Fingerprints, sir?'

'Might as well.' He waited until Spratt had been put through to Headquarters and had made his request. Then, seated at the desk, he began to fill his pipe.

'As far as we know, Dr. Peel was the last person to use that safe. Firth found it open. Not forced, either. So?'

'Either Dr. Peel omitted to close it, sir, or someone opened it who'd no right to touch it. In that case, it's a peterman's job. Not a top-line man, either, because there must be dozens of safe-breakers in the country who'd master an old-fashioned job like that one-handed. But, until we can be sure Peel himself didn't empty it . . .'

'In which case, if the idea was to remove all his secret stuff, why did he clear everything out of it?'

'Maybe as a blind, sir. Mrs. Brill says he took nothing from that safe home with him yesterday, but he could have done so previously.'

'So you're sold on Inspector Bates's theory of the sale of important stuff to a foreign power?' Hallam's expression was quizzical behind a wreath of smoke.

'I wouldn't say that, sir. But it's a possibility.'

'Maybe.' Hallam rose, stretching his limbs. 'Well, we'd better take some action. It's nearly ten, so the night security chaps will be here. We'll have a word with the man who's on duty in this block. Nip round to the porter's office, Jack, and — Hold on a minute.' Brisk knuckles were beating on the door panels. 'Come in!'

A police motor-cyclist stepped into the room, his crash helmet swinging by the straps from two fingers.

'Chief Inspector Hallam, sir?'

'Yes.'

'Message from Northwood Police Station, sir.' He fumbled at a tight tunic pocket button. 'C.I.D. Headquarters said you'd probably be still here. They thought it best not to contact you by phone because the message would have to go through the university switchboard and . . . ' The button surrendered and a notebook was tugged into view. 'I was on stand-by duty, sir, so I was sent over with it.'

'Right. Let's have it, then.'

' 'Message received, nine forty-six, from Mrs. Hazel Peel of Ashlea, Churchill Road, Deniston, 14.' Message reads, 'My husband has just rung me up from London, from a call-box. He said he was all right but might not be able to get in touch with me for a day or two. And that I mustn't bother Charles with any calls. I asked him what he was doing and what it was all about and he said not to worry, it was something he couldn't discuss, he sent his love and rang off.' '

'Thanks. No, wait a moment,' Hallam added as the constable turned to leave. 'What's your name?'

'Perkins, sir.'

'And you're on stand-by duty at Northwood? Nip out to your bike, call

116

your station and ask if I can send you on a further message — take you about half-an-hour.'

'Sir!' Perkins clattered out and Hallam looked across at Spratt, who was studying the shorthand transcript of the message he had put down in his own notebook.

'Jack, we've got to find out what this Dr. Peel is up to. That'll mean the Yard. But I think we can play it quietly, work a sort of semi-official routine, and a line from me to Browning might do the trick. We'll send Howard down there. He'll be at home now, won't he?'

'Should be, sir. When he rang in I told him to get off home but to stand by there.'

'Good. He can catch the night train down. Have a look next door, in the secretary's office, will you? See if you can find paper and envelopes, there should be some around.'

Spratt was back within a minute. 'Just the job, sir, a nice stationery rack on her desk. Mostly headed paper but I found some blank sheets.'

'Right. You know Howard's address? That's fine. Scribble him a note, tell him to get off to London tonight and contact Chief Superintendent Browning at the Yard tomorrow morning. You can tell him what it's all about. Meanwhile, I'll write a line to Browning myself.'

Constable Perkins, returning with the news that he was free to assist Chief Inspector Hallam, found the two C.I.D. plying biro pens with concentrated industry. Hallam glanced up to say, 'Shan't be a minute,' and went back to work.

'There, Perkins,' he said when the envelopes were addressed and sealed. 'Both of them to this address. Give them to Detective Constable Howard personally. Okay?'

Perkins glanced at the envelope which Spratt had written. 'I can get across there in ten minutes, sir. Shall I report back here?'

'If you would. Just so we know Howard has seen his orders.'

Perkins almost collided with the two

men who were entering the room.

'Ah,' Hallam said. 'The dab-men arrive. Show them where to operate, will you, sergeant? Then join me at the head porter's office.'

8

The head porter's office was now occupied by a round-faced, cheerful-looking man with a bald head and twinkling pale blue eyes.

'Handley, sir,' he introduced himself. 'Sam Handley. Alf Carr, the day man, told me about the spot of trouble in Metallurgy, before he went off duty. Something I can do for you, sir?'

'The safe over yonder — there's some doubt as to when it was opened. I'd like to see your security man who covers that block.'

'That'll be Bert Hackitt, sir. The chaps haven't begun their proper rounds yet. They'll be in the rest room. I'll get Hackitt up here at once.'

He hurried off, whistling softly. When voices and footsteps announced Handley's return with the guard, Hallam's mouth twisted in a grin of anticipation.

He was not disappointed. The guard,

heavily-built, with a thatch of greying hair, took one quick glance at the chief inspector and then pressed forward with hand thrust out and a grin to match Hallam's own.

'Bill! By heck, it's been a long time!'

They grasped hands warmly, while the head porter beamed upon them from the background.

'You two know each other, then? But, of course, you very well might, Bert being a retired policeman.'

'He taught me all I knew when I was a beat constable, but that's long ago now, Mr. Handley. Look, I'd like Bert to go across to Metallurgy with me. We can talk there. All right by you?'

'Of course, sir. Just do as you wish. I only hope that safe business'll turn out to be a day job, which'll mean we shan't have to worry!'

Hackitt frowned as they left the vestibule together.

'What's all this about then, Bill?'

'Time enough for that when we get over there. Tell me, how are things with you?'

They walked slowly, linking up with a past which now seemed very remote to both of them. Hallam remembered his old friend as an excellent type of the Uniformed Branch; he had been content to stay in it till he retired with sergeant's rank. This, Hackitt told him, had happened two years previously. Like most of his profession, he had looked out for another job. This one at the university was suiting him fine.

They met Spratt on the steps of the Science Faculty building and the sergeant was introduced and turned back with them. In Peel's office Hackitt learnt the essential facts.

'We've got to cover a period from last Friday, Bert, when Mrs. Brill went to the safe and closed it after her. Have you been on night-duty over that period?'

'I have.' Hackitt spoke slowly. 'I've done my rounds as usual, and seen nothing out of place in this building.'

Hallam looked at him sharply, but before he could put another question, Storrey, the fingerprint expert, came out of the store room, followed by his assistant.

'I've news for you, Mr. Hallam. That safe has been wiped cleaner than clean. There isn't a print on it. And that doesn't need an explanatory footnote, does it?'

'It certainly doesn't,' Hallam agreed. 'So it was opened illegally. Right, that'll do for you, then. And thanks.'

Storrey and his mate wished them all good night and left. Spratt cleared his throat.

'That lets Dr. Peel out, doesn't it, sir? If he'd cleared the safe, he'd have no reason to clean his prints off. I'm just wondering about Howard going to London, and if that'll be necessary now.'

'I think it will, Jack. I could do with knowing what this mysterious game is he seems to be playing. And we have to keep in mind we've a murder job on our hands. We've got to find out if, or if not, Peel was involved in that. He could have been. We've no proof yet he actually went to London yesterday.' He looked up at Hackitt. 'I'm talking freely,

Bert — before an ex-member of the Force.'

'I get you, Bill. I read about that killing in the evening paper. Of course, Penn Road is right out of my parish here. You'll have seen Molloy, though.'

'We have and he couldn't help. He seemed quite an alert type, too. Not likely to let much get by him.'

'Oh, Molloy's all right — I suppose.'

'Right. Now, then. Let's assume somebody else, not Dr. Peel, opened and cleared out that safe. Let's assume it was done during the hours when these premises were unoccupied. What have you got to say about that, Bert?'

Hackitt scratched his chin. 'You'll probably know each of us guards have a biggish area to cover. I mean, we can't keep everywhere under observation every minute of the night. I've done what I've had to since Friday last, by which I mean I've never skipped any of my rounds. I've seen nothing out of place here. That I'll swear to.'

'You can get into all these rooms, I suppose?' Spratt asked.

'Oh, yes. We've got to have means of ingress, in case of fire and so on, you know.'

'If this was an outside job, then, would any keys, I mean those carried by the other guards, fit these doors?'

'They wouldn't,' Hackitt answered promptly. 'That I do know. There's another point. Sometimes, you know, people are a bit careless. Yale locks are used throughout this university, but on odd occasions folks go home without dropping the latch behind 'em when they close a door. That hasn't happened here for a very long time — I can vouch for it. As an old beat copper, I try the handle of every door as I pass it, out of sheer force of habit, I suppose.'

'I'm glad you mentioned that,' Hallam said. 'And while we're on the subject of keys, what's the method you guards have when you come on duty? Does the head porter dish them out to each man?'

'No. They're on a board in his office. We take our own keys off their particular numbered hooks.'

'You say you've a big round to do.

Doesn't that mean carrying a load of keys?'

Hackitt thrust a hand into his pocket and brought out a ring which held a pair of keys only.

'When you came into this block you might have noticed a small office place just on the left of the entrance. That's where the day porter operates from. In that little office there's a duplicate set of keys for every room in this building. All I need is the key to the outer door and one to the small office. You follow me?

'I've three of these big blocks to do, and so I carry three rings, two keys on each. It's a simple system, but it works.'

'Right. Now, let's go back a bit, Bert. A few minutes ago you said that since last Friday you'd seen nothing out of place in this building.'

Hackitt nodded. 'That's so. Nothing at all.' He frowned. 'Look here, Bill. It could be possible, if this job was done during the night, that I could have been watched and as soon as my back was turned, somebody . . . They'd have to have been hiding in this building, though. I drop the front door latch as soon as I come in.' He rose from his chair. 'Mind if I have a look at that safe? I used to reckon to know a bit about 'em once.'

'Show him, Jack.' Hallam's lips tightened as he watched the pair of them enter the store room. His old friend Bert Hackitt was uneasy about something.

The inspection was very brief. Hackitt returned to his chair, grunting disgustedly.

'About as safe as a cardboard box without a lid! A peterman wouldn't even need a stethoscope to hear those tumblers falling. D'you remember Benny Clegg?'

'I do. And the last time I heard of Benny he'd got seven for a fur-warehouse job.'

'That's right, but he's out now. As it happens, I ran across him only a week or two ago. He told me he'd retired, he was getting too old for his profession. But, you know, this lot smells just like Benny to me. Benny invariably concealed himself in the place he was going to do. That's what I reckon happened here.'

'If I remember rightly, Benny only touched furs and jewels.'

'He might have changed. He's getting too old for a real craftsman's job, perhaps, but he'd do a thing like that yonder in his sleep. You could easily contact him, he's still on weekly report.'

'Maybe we'll do that. See who it is, Jack, will you?' Somebody was knocking at the office door.

Spratt went out, closing the door behind him. Hallam spoke quickly.

'This is a big job, Bert. As I've said, that killing is possibly involved. Don't hold anything back, will you?'

A flush rose into Hackitt's cheeks but he was spared an immediate reply. Spratt returned, with some sheets of paper in his hand.

'That was Perkins back. He's seen Howard and delivered the orders. Howard sent this report along. Apparently it deals with his movements at Price's garage this afternoon.' He slipped the sheets between the pages of his notebook. 'I've sent Perkins back to base. We didn't need him again, did we?'

Hallam shook his head. He turned to Hackitt.

'You were going to tell me, Bert . . . ?'

The ex-sergeant's jaw tightened. 'Oh, yes. About the incident last night.' He cleared his throat harshly. 'You may have noticed the tower with the clock on the building next to this one. What they call Central Building. It's where all the big bugs operate from — Vice-Chancellor's suite of rooms, Bursar's office, Senate meeting hall, and so on. It's a great game among the students to climb up to the clock. Absolutely forbidden, of course, but it is done now and then at nights, usually with a roped party. The big idea is to shove the clock hands on an hour, just to prove you've made it. Well, last night when I came out of here, about half-past ten it would be, I saw three of the young devils at it. They were about half-way up, all together on a ledge and getting ready for the next pitch.'

'You didn't see them when you came in here?'

'No, because the start of the climb is from the back of Central Building, over a lower roof and on to the front. Well, of course I could see them then, and I shouted at them to come down. One of 'em yelled back and told me what I could do with myself.

'I wasn't going to let 'em get away with that so I told 'em if they wouldn't be sensible I'd have the Fire Service here to fetch 'em down in less than no time. And then they would be in trouble. They had a bit of a conference and then the one who'd spoken before said okay, I'd won, and they'd come down. They started to move off the ledge.

'I went round to the back of Central, where I knew they'd have to come down, to see they all got safe to ground, which they did. I stepped out to them as they were unroping themselves, and the same lad as before asked me if I was going to report them. I said not that time, but if there was any more of it I'd see they suffered. They all had the decency to thank me and I saw them off the premises.'

He stopped, and relaxed in his chair, as if he were glad that was over and done with. Hallam thought for a moment.

'You've changed a bit in your old age,

Bert,' he said. 'I remember, when I first started and you were taking me round, you used to drum it into me — never let an offender off. If you do, ten to one he'll be on the same game again before long, and worse the second time. Besides, he won't respect you for it.'

For the second time Hackitt's weather-beaten face flushed.

'I'm still of that opinion. I broke my own rule in this case against my better judgement. I'm telling you now because I realize, thinking about it, that those lads had a damn good view from up there. On the ledge, they'd be looking straight along Penn Road, and that's where this killing was. It's possible they may have seen something.' He grinned wryly. 'I hope to God they didn't, however.'

'You're thinking, if they did, it'll have to come out that you failed to report them, Bert?'

A flash of surprise lit Hackitt's face.

'So it will, by damn! Hadn't thought of that. No, that wasn't it. No,' he repeated, 'it's one of those three I was hoping to keep out of trouble. I know him, you see.

One of my neighbours' lads.' He turned towards Spratt. 'Peter Shaw, 14 Helsey View, Deniston 6, Sergeant. You see, Bill, the lad's a polio cripple with one leg badly affected. He's had a hard struggle, but he wouldn't let it beat him. Did well at school and going on fine here, I'm told. Rules or no rules, Bill, you can't make more trouble for a chap like that.'

'I'm afraid we'll have to see him, though. The fact is, Bert, we've no line at all on the Penn Road case. What about Shaw's companions? Do you know them?'

Hackitt shook his head. 'One was red-haired, with a scrubby beard. He was the cheeky one. The third was a tall, very thin youth with receding hair and glasses. Young Shaw would probably give you their names if you pushed him.'

'Looks as though we'll have to.' Hallam got up. 'I can't see us doing any more good here tonight. I think we'll get on and see Shaw now, Jack. Then we'll pack it up for the day. And thanks, Bert. We'll leave you to shut up here.'

They returned to their car and made

good speed through the evening-quiet cross streets to reach a dual carriageway which gave Spratt an opportunity to comment.

'I had a look at that clock-tower ledge when we came out, sir. The thought of a sound man, with climbing experience, up there was bad enough, but a cripple! You'd say it was impossible!'

'Apparently it didn't prove so. You can see why young Shaw tried it, though.'

'Oh, sure! He wanted to prove he could, in spite of his disability. And I'm not blaming him for it. I reckon it's the only way people — especially young people — can come to terms with a physical handicap. They've just got to show themselves it's not going to beat them. But I do blame the two who were with him. They never should have encouraged him to try it.'

Hallam muttered his agreement and then was silent until they found Helsey View. It was part of a suburb of middle-class houses, semi-detached, lining the street on each side in a double, box-like row. Each had its square of front garden and the grass verges in front of the fences were well kept.

A man in his shirt sleeves answered their knock.

'Mr. Shaw?' Hallam continued, at the man's nod, 'I am Detective Chief Inspector Hallam of the Deniston Police and this is Detective Sergeant Spratt. Is your son Peter at home? We'd like to talk to him.'

Shaw stood squarely in the doorway, peering at them. Transport inspector? Works foreman? Small businessman? He could be any of them, Hallam thought.

'What's up, then? Why d'you want to see Peter? It's a bit late, too, isn't it?'

'As he's at the university, and we are carrying out investigations there, we think he may be able to help us.'

The man stepped aside. 'I can't imagine how he can do that. You'd better come in. The wife's gone to bed, so we'll go in here.' He led the way to a dining room which had the air of a place very seldom used.

'Coldest spot in the house, this,' Shaw

muttered. He switched on an electric fire which stood in the hearth. 'Peter's in his bedroom, studying. Can't get him to bed early. I'll fetch him down.'

The fair-haired young man who came into the room, dragging his left leg awkwardly, had handsome features and clear, steady eyes. He looked from Hallam to Spratt.

'My dad says you wish to talk to me. Won't you sit down?'

'Ah, of course.' His father pulled out chairs. 'I'll stay in on this, if you don't mind.'

'Of course.' Hallam smiled, and spoke to the younger man. 'What we're interested in are your university activities of last night, Mr. Shaw. Which could make it a little awkward, your father being present now.'

Peter Shaw laughed. 'If you're referring to that stunt on Central, dad knows all about it. The night-guard — Mr. Hackitt — said he wouldn't report us, but just in case he changed his mind I thought it best to get my own story in to dad first. Though we haven't told mum. I do hope she won't have to know. She's a prize worrier.'

'Daft young idiot, he is,' the elder Shaw growled. 'Doing a senseless thing like that. Could have broken his neck. Half-way up that tower, he was.' But the note of pride in his voice cancelled out the reproof. 'Don't tell me you've come to arrest him for breaking university rules?'

'Not this time, Mr. Shaw.' Hallam gestured to a chair and the youth seated himself awkwardly. 'Last night a member of the university staff was killed, in a house in Penn Road.'

'It's in the paper,' Peter Shaw said promptly. 'Man named Bradley, wasn't it? I didn't know him, of course. I do physics.'

'Well, here's the point,' Hallam continued. 'It's quite possible his death could have taken place about the time you were on that clock tower. I understand you get a clear view along Penn Road from there. Did you see anything unusual, anybody going or coming along Penn Road, especially out of one of the houses?'

Peter Shaw laughed. 'Me? I was far too scared to look anywhere except at the wall just in front of my eyes. I daren't even glance down. I certainly never took a sight along Penn Road.'

'Maybe one or other of your companions did so?'

'That I wouldn't know. You'll have to ask — ' He broke off. 'Do you know who they were?'

'We don't. But as we shall have to talk to them, we need to ask you for their names.'

Peter Shaw's lips tightened. 'Sorry, but nothing doing. You've got on to me through Mr. Hackitt, who recognized me. Obviously, a promise means nothing to him. That's by the way. The point is, I don't tattle on my pals.'

'We've got a good description of them,' Hallam said mildly. 'And, let me tell you, Mr. Hackitt only gave us the story of last night because of one thing. He realized that in a murder investigation time is important, and he considered his promise didn't hold because of that. We can find these other fellows, but it won't be done

137

in a hurry. I'm appealing to your intelligence, you see.'

'He's right, of course.' The elder Shaw banged a fist on the table. 'You've got to help, Peter, in every way you can.'

Obstinacy seeped from the young face.

'Yes, I suppose so.' He saw Spratt's opening notebook and pushed himself round in his chair to face the sergeant. 'There was Dennis Ryle — he's doing geography, but I haven't the faintest idea where he lives — in digs somewhere, I think. And Gerry Dickson, in physics, same year as myself. He's at Monkbridge House, that new students' residence in Wellingborough Road.'

'Thank you. Any questions from you, sergeant?'

'I'm just a bit interested in this climbing stunt, sir. Naturally, there'd be some organization of it. Is there any reason why it took place last night?'

Hallam said, 'Ah, yes,' and looked at Peter Shaw. 'Give us the details, will you?'

'It's quite simple. Some time early last week I was in the Union, talking to Dennis Ryle. He's the president of the

Climbing Club — they go all over the place, rock climbing, and of course, he's an absolute expert. I' — he looked down at the table — 'I envy him, rather. Would have liked to have done that sort of thing myself.

'Anyway, Gerry Dickson came up and he asked Dennis if it was a fact he'd done the clock tower climb. Dennis admitted he had, in his first year. He said it wasn't all that difficult solo and with a roped party, just a piece of cake. Gerry said he was mad keen to try it and would Dennis take him up? Dennis wasn't at all sold on the idea, but Gerry never takes no for an answer, and at last got him persuaded. And all the time they were arguing I was standing there, looking like a kid with his nose pressed to a sweetshop window, I suppose. Gerry said how about taking me up, too? Dennis sort of looked at me as if he knew what I was thinking, and he laughed and said right, if I was game. Of course, I was.

'We discussed when and Gerry said he couldn't make it till the following Monday — last night. That was all right with me and Dennis said it would give him the chance to put us through a bit of practice. On Thursday afternoon we went out to Dragon Crag with ropes. Dennis fixed it so that Gerry was first on the rope last night, with Dennis giving him directions, me in the middle and Dennis last — control leader, he called himself.' Peter Shaw laughed suddenly. 'I'm glad we didn't do the whole route. I'd had plenty when we got to that ledge. Still . . . '

'Still,' Hallam echoed, 'you did jolly well, lad. And I don't think we shall have to trouble you again.

'And that's about all for today,' he added as they left the house. 'We'll see the other two tomorrow. I hope they saw something.'

Spratt nodded and held out the car keys.

'Do you mind driving back, sir? I'd like to read Howard's report again.'

He folded back the report sheets as the car moved away. A minute went by. Then,

'Ah, here it is. Gerald Dickson, student. Howard ran across him at Price's garage this afternoon. Didn't like him much, either. Then later, he saw Dickson meet some chap or other . . . Ford Pop — ZE 606. Now where have I seen that number recently?'

He was still puzzling over it when, at Headquarters, Hallam wished him good night.

9

Hallam pushed the last of the Wednesday morning crime reports to one side.

'Nothing urgent there, praise be. So we can concentrate on this university job, or jobs. I'm ready, Jack, to hear all the brilliant ideas which have come to you during the night.'

Spratt grunted. 'No brilliance, sir. I'm just wishing we could find the object which was first used on Bradley. Here's Dr. Ransome's detailed report. The old blunt instrument was apparently laid against Bradley's skull with some force. The smoothing iron was used to finish the job.'

'So the killer was taking no chances. Does anything strike you about the three possible suspects we have — Markham, who stole from Firth's room and later returned the loot at Bradley's insistence, Crayston who was lent money he was preparing to pay back, and Dr. Peel, known to have had a row with Bradley over the article in the students' newspaper?'

'None of them has a sound motive for killing Bradley, sir. Markham admits to a quick temper, but his alibi seems all right. Unless he'd done a second steal which Bradley knew about, which either hasn't been discovered yet, or hasn't been reported. There are those things from Peel's safe, of course.'

'Maybe we could do with a recheck on Markham's alibi . . . Two crimes in the same locality on the same night. Are they connected? It seems to me we've got to assume they are. And that Bradley knew of the other one and was killed before he could use his knowledge of it.'

'As far as we know,' Spratt argued, 'Bradley was in his room all the time, waiting for this fellow Humpkin, who hasn't been traced yet, though I think I know where he is.'

Interest gleamed in Hallam's eyes. 'That's something, anyway. What do you mean?'

'That man who was knocked down, late

on Monday evening, in Harlow Street, by a car which didn't stop. No identification.'

'I remember.'

'Being extra busy yesterday, we didn't follow that job up. But Howard put in a report last night, along with the one re his garage visit. There was no identification possible at the hospital from the clothes or contents of pockets. I rang up just now and the patient is still unconscious. They've had no inquiries about a missing person, nor have we. I wouldn't mind betting it's Humpkin who's lying there. He isn't a local man, or somebody would have been asking about him, likely as not.'

'It's a possibility, I suppose. Nothing's turned up from the registers-of-electors checks?'

As Spratt shock his head Hallam called, 'Come in!' and a constable obeyed. He carried a large manilla envelope.

'This has just come for you, sir. From the university. They sent a messenger with it. He had been told there was no need to wait for an answer.'

'Right, Madison.' Hallam took the

envelope. It was addressed to him in large, sprawling handwriting. He shook out its contents. There was a note, in the same sprawl, on university-headed paper and an opened envelope addressed to Edmund Bradley, Esk., Regional History Institute, 2 Penn Road, Deniston, 2. This contained two different pieces of note-paper. One of them made Hallam draw a quick breath.

'Talk of the devil, Jack! Come and look at this.'

With Spratt at his shoulder, Hallam read the covering note.

'Dear Hallam,

The enclosed letter, addressed to Bradley, arrived in this morning's mail. In the circumstances, I felt justified in opening it. It contained a second sheet, also enclosed. As this second item, from Bradley himself, is to one Humpkin, of whom you were inquiring here yesterday, I felt you should have it as soon as possible.

Regards,

Kenneth Kirk.'

Hallam took up the letter addressed to Bradley. It was headed 8 Harlow Street and dated the previous day.

'Dear Sir,
When going to work this morning I picked up a letter in the road outside my house. Seeing the letter was from you I am sending it back. I picked it up some little distance away from where an accident happened last night when a man was knocked down by one of these hit-and-run drivers. I thought it might be the injured man that dropped the letter. It has got a bit smudged owing to last night's rain and wind.
Yours faithfully,
Leonard Routh.'

'Not everybody would take as much trouble as that,' Hallam commented as he flattened out the letter which Bradley had written.

Like Kirk's note, it was on official university paper. The writing was small, precise and clear despite its exposure to the weather.

'Dear Mr. Humpkin,

I am delighted to know you will be able to come to Deniston on Monday next and am looking forward to our meeting. I quite understand the circumstances which will make your arrival a late one, but this will be of no inconvenience to me at all. I suggest you come straight to the university from the bus station, as the distance is less than half a mile, and the way much easier to find than to my own flat.' Here followed directions and a sketch map. The letter concluded. 'I shall not hear of your putting up at an hotel for the night. I shall be delighted to fix you up in my own rooms.

Most cordially yours,

Edmund Bradley.'

'Yes,' Hallam said. 'Your guess looks like being right, Jack. Humpkin was walking across from the bus station. He had the letter in his hand, checking his route. See, he had been told to come by Harlow Street. Probably he was knocked down as he started to cross it. The letter

147

was blown some way along the street. I think it may tell us why Bradley was killed. I don't think he remained in his room all the time he was waiting for Humpkin. I mean, would you?'

'No,' Spratt said thoughtfully. 'Time went on, Humpkin didn't arrive. Bradley became impatient, worried perhaps that his visitor has missed his way. He went out into Penn Road looking for him. Probably strolled around quite a bit in case Humpkin had got lost in that maze of university buildings. Bradley could have seen something he wasn't meant to see. So he was killed to shut his mouth.'

'Killed in his own room, remember, Jack. And no signs of a struggle. We can postulate he knew the killer, was finished off while in conversation with him. And the only 'something' Bradley could have seen, one imagines, had to do with the looted safe in the science building. It all hangs together but it's pure theory. We've nothing to support it.'

'Trouble is, sir, theory is the only thing we have to work on yet.' He grinned. 'That was one fact which didn't get into the papers this morning. They've all spread themselves on the killing, as you'll have seen ... I suppose we'll still be keeping the safe robbery under cover?'

'Until it's been proved to have been robbed, yes. For all we know, Peel emptied it. He had every right to do so.' Hallam pushed away from his desk and stood up. 'Shove this lot in the file, Jack. There are these two students, Ryle and Dickson, to see.'

But one of the mountains had already come to Mahomet. They were passing the counter of the main office when the man on duty halted Hallam.

'Excuse me, sir, I was just going to send through. There's a Dennis Ryle asking to see you. University student — he said you'd have heard of him.' He motioned towards a line of chairs in the corridor beyond the desk.

'Thanks.' Hallam went forward to a man seated on one of the chairs. 'Mr. Ryle? I'm Detective Chief Inspector Hallam.'

Ryle swung easily to his feet. He was older than the average student — Hallam guessed twenty-eight at least — and in spite of his spectacles and rapidly-thinning brown hair he looked muscular and fit. He had a self-confident manner and spoke quickly.

'I saw Peter Shaw at the university this morning, sir,' he told Hallam. 'We both had early lectures. I cut mine because Shaw said you'd probably want to talk to me. I'd prefer such talking to be done here.'

'So would I, Mr. Ryle. I'm glad you came. We'll go to my office with Detective Sergeant Spratt here. This won't take more than a few minutes.'

Spratt found the caller a chair and went to his own corner desk. As Hallam seated himself Dennis Ryle said, 'Let's get the sermon over first, shall we?'

'Sermon, Mr. Ryle? I'm not with you.'

'What? No rocket for breaking the university regulations, taking a handicapped man on a dangerous climb — all that?'

'Not our business. Not even to report your — er — escapade.'

'Escapade!' Ryle laughed shortly. 'That

makes it sound all very childish for a man of my age, and in my final year, too. But the fact was — oh, well!' He spread his hands. 'Look. I play cricket and tennis. Badminton, too. I'm a distance runner, a mountaineer, and I swim. When I see a chap with a handicap like Shaw's, I realize how damned lucky I am, and he was aching to prove he could do something athletic. Actually, that tower climb's a doddle. It has a reputation it doesn't deserve. And even though we only got part of the way, if you could have seen Shaw's face when we got there!'

Hallam nodded sympathetically. 'I understand. But what we're interested in is what you may have seen besides Shaw's look of triumph.'

'Ah, yes. He told me about that this morning. And I did see a man wandering around. He came from the Penn Road direction. Shortish — that's all I can say. I only saw his figure, you see.'

'I'd like every detail you can give me, Mr. Ryle.'

'Dickson had just reached the ledge which proved to be the end of the climb. I made sure he was belayed on to a side pinnacle there and I sent Shaw up. Shaw climbed slowly, of course, but quite safely. I was standing in a guttering between two pieces of roofing with nothing to do but pay out Shaw's rope. It was about then I saw the man turn out of the end of Penn Road and come towards the main buildings. He was walking slowly, looking about him. Shaw called down to say he was on the ridge and I followed him quickly there. I didn't see the man again.'

'Very clearly told, Mr. Ryle. I believe you had just reached the ridge when the guard spotted you?'

'Yes, and that was Dickson's fault. If he'd kept quiet the man wouldn't have seen us, and he probably would never have looked up. Dickson said, in a sort of startled, exclaiming tone, 'Hell, that's done it. We're for it now!' or words to that effect. The guard looked up and ordered us down. Even then Dickson had to give him some cheek. And on the said way down Shaw was worried. The guard knew him, you see. But as it turned out, that was all for the best because, to save Shaw trouble, the man promised to say nothing. We all cleared off our separate ways and I didn't see the Penn Road man, or anybody else, on my way out. That's the lot.'

Spratt laid his pencil down. 'There's just one point before you go, Mr. Ryle. I understand it was Dickson who suggested the climb and persuaded you to take them?'

'Why, yes. I wasn't at all keen at first, you know. Dickson came to me afterwards, privately, and apologized for pushing me into the business. He said he was a pal of Shaw's, and he knew how keen Peter was to have a go. I saw his point.'

'And it was Dickson who set the date and time?'

'Yes, again. Is all this significant?'

'It's just that we like to get a clear picture, sir.'

'I wish I could have been of greater help to you.'

'You've done very well, and thank you,' Hallam said, and sat thoughtfully at his desk while Spratt saw the student out.

The sergeant returned, grinning.

'What price pure theory now, sir? It's as I — er — we said, Bradley got tired of waiting for Humpkin, came out to look for him. He saw what he shouldn't have, was followed back and killed.'

'If we accept that, we also accept the theory that both crimes up yonder were connected. Right?'

'Looks like it, to me.'

'And that Peel wasn't the one who cleared the safe?'

Spratt hesitated. 'I see what you're getting at, sir. We've got to mark time on that angle until we get hold of Peel. Fair enough. So it's Dickson next? Right, sir. I'm interested in Dickson. I — ' He stopped so abruptly on his way to the door that Hallam almost collided with him.

'That Ford Popular car, registration ZE 606, mentioned in Howard's report. I've just remembered where I've seen it. It was standing outside Molloy's house when we called to interview him!'

'Which may, or may not be, significant,' Hallam returned. 'We can open up that line with Dickson, anyway. We'll try his living quarters first.'

Monkbridge House, in Wellingborough Road, was claimed to be the ultimate in residential accommodation for students. Everything was laid on, from garages for the students' cars and motor-cycles, to electrically-controlled roasting spits in the communal kitchens. Knowing that the man they sought was just one of a population of two hundred and fifty at Monkbridge House, the C.I.D. men made their first call at the bursar's office for further details. They learnt that Gerald Dickson was housed in Block C, 4th Floor, Room 6.

The fourth floor was the top one. Speed lifts were provided in each block, and the detectives used the one in Block C.

They stepped out on to a rubber-floored corridor lined with numbered doors. Spratt tapped at Number Six. There was immediate movement inside and the two glanced at each other with satisfaction. The door opened and a red-haired, red-bearded young man of slight build, wearing an open-necked blue shirt and greasy jeans, looked at them inquiringly.

'Mr. Gerald Dickson?' The red head nodded.

'We are police officers.' Hallam gave their names, but not before he had marked the consternation in the student's eyes, the tightening of his grip on the edge of the door.

'And you're wanting me, are you? Whatever for?'

'Wouldn't it be better if we talked inside?'

'Of course.' He stood back. 'There isn't a lot of room, I'm afraid.'

There was a rexine-covered seat which topped a bunk bed, with a set of lockers above it. A large desk, loaded with books and papers, was set in front of the wide window, and two doors, both ajar, showed a fitted wardrobe and a toilet with washbasin and shower. Dickson indicated the bed seat and Hallam and Spratt lowered themselves upon it. Their host swung the revolving desk chair to face them. He sat down uneasily, as if the chair had been upholstered with barbed wire.

'Well, what is all this?'

'Nothing to get alarmed about, Mr. Dickson.'

'Who said I was alarmed? I mean, I've done nothing to have you people after me.' A quick frown creased his forehead. 'Here, is it something to do with Evan Price?'

'Now, whyever should you think that?' Hallam asked.

'Well, because — ' He pulled himself up. 'Well, I mean, I go there occasionally — the money's useful — and — and — well, you know yourselves that garages have to carry out all sorts of regulations and — well, we get you chaps in asking about accidents and stolen cars and so on. You know what it is.' He wiped the palms of his hands on his jeans.

'At the moment,' Hallam said, 'we aren't concerned with Mr. Price's activities. We — '

Dickson broke in on him. His voice was pitched higher now.

'Oh, of course! This place has become a real hotbed of crime, hasn't it? Some old guy gets knocked off on Monday

157

night, and — ' His teeth clamped on his lips.

'Yes, Mr. Dickson? And — ?'

'And so, I suppose,' Dickson said quickly, 'you have to go around questioning everybody. I can't help you myself, though.'

'We think there's a chance you can. Just cast your mind back to Monday evening, please. I'm sure you'll remember what you were doing then.'

Dickson stared at them, drawing a long breath.

'You mean the tower climb? I see. So the guard bloke split after all, did he? But surely that's not a police matter?'

Hallam explained why they were there and as he talked Dickson's chair seemed to become more comfortable. He settled back in it and scratched at his immature beard thoughtfully.

'As Dennis Ryle told you, I led the climb. Under his direction, of course. I was on that ledge for quite a while before Peter joined me. Dennis was telling Peter just what to do and I knew, if he slipped, I would have to hold him. Naturally, I was watching him carefully. I hadn't much opportunity for enjoying the general view.' He shook his head decisively. 'No, come to think of it, I saw nothing, and nobody walking about.'

'We had to check,' Hallam told him. At his side Spratt moved restlessly. Hallam turned to him. 'Something you want to say, sergeant?'

'Yes, sir. Mr. Dickson here, as he tells us, saw nothing while on the ledge. I believe, though, sir, it was you who first saw the security guard.'

Dickson grinned sourly. 'Oh, him. Yes, I did, and I lost my head a bit about that. As Dennis told me afterwards, if I'd kept quiet he'd probably never have seen us. Matter of fact, Peter Shaw wasn't too comfortable on the ledge and I was getting a bit worried about him. That's why I didn't sort of think — about the guard, I mean.'

'You know the guard, Hackitt, personally, Mr. Dickson?'

'Me? Not at all. Peter knew him. I believe they live in the same street, or something.'

'I think you're acquainted with one of Hackitt's colleagues, however, sir? A man named Molloy?'

Dickson sat very still. 'Molloy,' he repeated after some moments of silence. 'Molloy. No, I don't think I know him. I mean, why should I?'

'You were at Price's garage in Willow Street yesterday afternoon, sir?'

'I was. I had a free afternoon.' He beat one hand on his knee. 'Oh, yes! And one of your plainclothes man came in, asking about Markham, who also works there now and then.'

'Quite. And soon afterwards the detective constable saw you in conversation with Molloy, on the piece of waste ground behind the garage.'

'Did he, now? So this Molloy must be the chap who runs a Ford Popular — would he be dark-haired with an Irish accent?'

'That fits his description, sir. Are you telling us you didn't know him by name?'

'Sure. I don't know every casual motorist who pulls in at Taff's place for a service or a repair. Taff does a cash trade

160

— he won't let customers run up bills. They come and they go.'

'But Molloy didn't actually go to the garage yesterday. How was that?'

Dickson raised one foot to rest it across his knee. The fingers of his left hand began to play on the scuffed, dirt-encrusted leather of his pointed shoe.

'Look — sergeant, isn't it? — this could be a bit tricky for me. I wouldn't like it to get to Taff's ears. Point is, this Irish customer brought his Pop in for a repair. Horn wasn't working. I was told to look at the job and I found a faulty electrical connection. I put it right, as I thought, the bloke paid up and drove off. That would be — oh, something like a week ago. Then, yesterday, he rang in. I took the call. The horn had gone wrong again and he was playing merry hell about it. Now, I didn't want Taff to know I'd boobed on the job, so I told this character if he'd bring the car in again, we'd see to it, but as we were full to the doors, would he drive on to the empty patch and I'd come out to him there. I fixed a time, when I could say I was going out for

161

some tea, met the bloke, put my former bit of carelessness right and off he drove, happy as Larry. So he turns out to be on the security staff, eh? Pure coincidence.'

'He lives on the other side of town from Willow Street, sir. Odd he should go so far to find a garage.'

Dickson shrugged. 'He could have been driving by, having found the horn was useless. Very likely we didn't look very busy just then — I don't know. He'd naturally want to get it fixed at once, from a legal point or view.' He let his foot slide to the ground. 'Okay, sergeant? Quite satisfied? Look, I don't want to be inhospitable, but I have this work to hand in today.'

Hallam rose from the bed, somewhat stiffly. 'You've given us all we want, Mr. Dickson, and thanks. We'll be on our way.'

The lift was on the ground floor so they used the stairs.

'Quick thinker, that lad,' Hallam said. 'But he didn't quite put it over. Don't you agree, Jack?'

'I do that, sir. And I'll bet I know where our next call will be. At Molloy's, before Dickson can get to him first. Am I right?'

'Hit it in one,' Hallam replied.

10

Arthur Howard enjoyed his journey to London. The midnight train from Deniston was half empty. He was able to find a compartment with only one other traveller in it, a quiet, untalkative man who observed the usual courtesies only before saying, 'Ah, well, nothing like it,' and stretching himself full length along the seat.

Before he himself settled down, Howard reviewed his own particular circumstances and found them very pleasing. Earlier, in the afternoon of that day, he had been in the depths of depression, now he was riding high. Hallam could have sent a sergeant, or one of the senior detective constables, on this job. True, his method, so Howard had been told, was always to keep the original team on a case, but here was an occasion when he might have been expected to break his rule. Very junior detective constables were not usually sent south to confer with the glamorous Yard. Unless, of course, they were, in Hallam's eyes, a good deal more promising than normal . . .

Steady on, young Howard, he rebuked himself. That's enough of that. You're on this job because it's a simple one, the sort any half-wit could do. In fact, come to think of it, it was odd that a man should have been sent down at all. Why not just ask the London lads to work it from their end?

He took out the note Sergeant Spratt had written to him and read it again under the shaded lamp. Contact a Dr. Peel, try such-and-such an address, ask him to get in touch with us immediately. Brief details on who and what Dr. Peel was. And a hint at the end that it was all a bit hush-hush, and to watch his step.

Howard put the note safely away with the envelope addressed by Hallam to Chief Superintendent Browning. He kicked off his shoes and got his head down. He didn't know how long this job would take, but he'd had the foresight to ring up a nice little bed-and-breakfast place in Coram Street. He'd booked a room there for the following night, so that was . . . was all . . . fixed . . . up.

He woke briefly once, was conscious the train had come to a halt somewhere, and settled himself to sleep again. The next time he opened his eyes it was to a grey dawn and to the sounds of a very big station indeed. He sat up. His companion had gone. Howard rubbed the misted window and recognized King's Cross. As he was lacing his shoes the door opened and a coloured porter put his head in.

'Now, boss, you'se here. Dis train don't go no furder.' He glanced at Howard's one small bag disgustedly, spat on the platform and turned away.

Howard got out of the train, stretching cramped muscles. Six o'clock, a grim time to arrive at a London station.

Half an hour later life began to take on a brighter tone. He'd washed and shaved and changed his shirt in one of the station's lavatories and was now sitting down to an excellently cooked, well-served breakfast in the restaurant.

He finished a third cup of tea, picked

up his bag and walked out into Euston Road. He turned along Upper Woburn Place and finally left into Coram Street. Yes, he was told, he could leave his bag and welcome, could have a second breakfast if he wished. Howard refused the offer, was given a key and went upstairs to dump his bag in the room he expected to occupy that night.

He had nearly an hour to kill, for he judged nine o'clock would be the correct time to present himself at the Yard. But an hour in London passes quickly to a provincial visitor, and, having decided to walk it, anyway, Howard found it was after nine when he turned from Northumberland Avenue along the Victoria Embankment.

He had his credentials ready, and found he needed them as he was passed from duty officer to duty officer. He finally arrived at a counter-like desk where a grey-haired sergeant peered through spectacles at the letter Hallam had written.

'Chief Super Browning, eh? And you want to see him?' He made Browning sound like one of the Sights of London. 'Well, I don't know as how you can, son. Where'd you say you were from?'

'C.I.D. Deniston Police.' Howard was getting tired of giving the same information.

'Deniston. That's up north, near Manchester, in't it?'

'It's miles from Manchester, on the other side of the Pennines.'

'Of course! I got yer now, boy. Second Division, near the bottom — that's it.' He looked at the envelope in his hand again. 'Who'd you say this was from?'

Howard told him. The sergeant said he'd ring through. He showed surprise at the telephone's reply.

'You're to go up at once, he says. Right, then. Through that door, up the stairs facing you, turn left along the corridor, fifth door. You'll see the name.'

When Howard had knocked at the fifth door and been bidden to enter, he walked into a large room with a wide window overlooking the river. One man sat behind a massive desk, facing the door. There were two other men, each at a desk, somewhat smaller, on which were telephones, constantly ringing. The man behind the large desk was large, too, with silver hair framing a round, bucolic-looking face. One hand beckoned Howard forward, the other was held out for Hallam's letter. The silver head nodded at a chair. Howard sat.

Browning picked up a slim paper knife and slit the envelope. He read Hallam's letter slowly. Then he looked up.

'So you're Detective Constable Howard. And how's crime in Deniston, Howard?'

'More of it than we want, sir.' Howard thought that was as good an answer as any. Browning smiled.

'Anyway, it's good to hear from an old friend again. We must see what we can do.' He raised his voice. 'Can you spare a minute, Tony?'

'I can if these phones will leave me alone, sir.' The man at one of the smaller desks pressed a switch and spoke into an intercom. 'Just hold everything for a few minutes, will you?' He got up and came forward, a lean, whippet-like person, small for a policeman.

'This is Detective Constable Howard from Deniston,' Browning said. 'Chief Inspector Amberley, Howard.' The young man had got smartly to his feet but Browning waved him down. 'Read that,' he told Amberley, who did, and clucked his tongue.

'Oh, no! Not another one of those, surely?'

'We hope not, Tony. Hallam thinks, you see — and I agree with him — that at the moment it's best kept as local business. That's why he's sent a man down. Can you fix up a mate for him?'

'I think so, sir.' Amberley looked at Howard. 'You know what you're here for? You've had definite and precise orders?'

'Yes, sir.'

'Right. Come with me. I'll detail somebody to assist you.'

Thus Howard made the acquaintance of Detective Constable Nick Glover, a merry-eyed young man who, it soon turned out, had little respect for authority and the minimum awe of regulations. He suggested they should start work by having a cup of coffee in the canteen.

'So you're from Deniston,' he said when they were seated at a canteen table. 'Pretty grim up there, ain't it?'

'How d'you mean?'

'Well — the weather, and all these pit heaps and that.'

'Deniston itself's a bit mucky,' Howard returned, 'but not so bad as London. It's getting spoilt, though, is Deniston.'

'In what way?'

'Too many southerners crowding the place nowadays. They come up to get good jobs and to enjoy the healthy air.'

Glover said, 'Is that a fact?' and seemed subdued for a few moments. Then, 'This job old Ambergris has put me on with you, we've got to be careful not to rush it. Watch your step, he says, for God's sake don't let it get to Ministry level, he says. So we'd better take time out to make a plan.'

Howard shrugged. 'It seems simple enough to me. I've been told to contact this Dr. Peel and we do that through his pal Mitchell. I've got his address. Saxby House, Belsize Street, Haverstock Hill. Flat 4b. How do we get there?'

'Belsize Park Station, Underground from Charing Cross,' Glover responded promptly. 'Won't take us long. What about another cup of coffee?'

But Howard, anxious to get to work, shook his head. He sat there impatiently while Glover, excusing himself, joined a small group of men who had just come in. For the best part of ten minutes Glover became the life and soul of the party.

However, when he did break it up, he seemed prepared at last to earn his pay. He set a cracking pace to Charing Cross Underground and on the way to Belsize Park he listened attentively while Howard told him all the details of Dr. Peel which Spratt had given him.

'There's no suggestion he's involved with a woman here, Arthur?' They were on Christian name terms by now.

'Not as far as I know. Anyway, he'd hardly rush off as he did if that was the lark, would he?'

'Likely not. Well, it's a question of shall we find this Mitchell at home or will it be a case of beating up for him wherever he works.'

But here they were lucky. Saxby House was a block of flats, expensive residences by the look of them. The lift to the fourth floor set them opposite 4b and when Glover knocked, footsteps approached and the door was flung open by a small, white-haired man in a dressing-gown. He glared ill-temperedly at them and Howard was reminded of a Jack Russell terrier with stomach-ache.

'Well? What is it? What d'you want?'

'Mr. Charles Mitchell, sir?'

'Of course, of course! Who else?'

'We are police officers, sir,' Glover said smoothly. 'Detective Constable Glover and' — he flicked a thumb — 'Detective Constable Howard, of the Deniston Criminal Investigation Department.' He rolled out the full title sonorously. The little man sniffed.

'I am charmed, I'm sure. I am also extremely busy.' The sentences were barked out explosively. 'What is it you want?'

'If we might come in a moment, sir?'

Mitchell nodded grudgingly. He turned

and preceded them across a tiny hall into a room which, at first glance, might have been part of a museum. Show cases lined the walls, there was a metal filing cabinet in one corner, a gate-legged table in the centre of the room was occupied by a large album and a litter of postage stamps and mounts.

'Nice place you have here, sir,' Glover said sociably. 'Most unusual, if I may say so. Unique, in fact.'

The Jack Russell almost wagged its tail now.

'You certainly may say so, officer. As will be obvious to you, I am a collector. I claim, with some justification, to have the finest collection of crested buttons in the world. Here!' He trotted towards a set of three large glass-fronted cabinets. 'Hunt buttons in this one, service buttons next, and this holds public transport and other buttons, including a number of police specimens. You may also be interested . . . '

Twenty minutes later they managed to get him back to earth, after a surfeit of snuff-boxes, postmarks, pens, pipes, Valentine cards, matchbox covers, crest china, horse brasses, watermarks and keys.

It was Howard who broached the subject of their call, for Nick Glover, having brought them there, now seemed content to step into the background.

'Ah,' Mitchell said, in a benign humour now. 'Lewis Peel. A most gifted young man. Known him for years. On the run, is he?'

'Oh, no, sir. But — in confidence, sir — some important papers were removed from Dr. Peel's safe at Deniston University, and we're anxious to contact him, so we can find out exactly what was taken.'

Mitchell had seated himself at the table, on the only chair in the room. He looked up at Howard and shook his head doubtfully.

'Odd, very odd, officer. I thought so myself. Lewis has always looked on this place as his pied-à-terre when he has come to London for conferences and such. He hates hotels. Can't blame him.'

He cleared his throat. 'But to resume.

Last night his wife rang me up. Said Lewis was in London and was he staying with me? I hadn't seen him and told her so. Later on she rang me again. She sounded worried, deucedly worried. Then, soon after, who should blow in but Lewis himself. He seemed worried, too. I mean by that he was all on edge, said he was on an important mission and rushed to death with it all. He asked me to call his wife and let her know he was all right and he gave me the Deniston number, wrote it on the back of a piece of paper he tore off a letter. I have it here.'

He thrust two fingers into a pocket of his dressing-gown. Howard stepped forward and took the scrap of paper from him.

'Then,' Mitchell went on, 'Lewis suddenly changed his mind and said he'd ring his wife himself later and he dashed off and I haven't seen him since.'

'So you've no idea where he is now, sir?'

Mitchell shook his head.

'I have given you all the information I

have.' He got up. 'I cannot help you further.'

Howard turned the piece of paper over in his fingers.

'We'd like to keep this, sir.'

'Of course, of course.' He moved quickly to the door and they followed him out. As Howard thanked him, he said:

'If Lewis appears again, I take it you would wish me to ask him to get in touch with the police?'

'If you would, sir.'

'Dead end, seemingly,' Glover remarked as they went down the stairs. 'Pity. I was hoping we could spin this job out a bit.'

Howard handed him the scrap of paper he had taken from Mitchell. 'Turn it over, Nick.'

On the other side was part of a printed address. The scrap had obviously been torn from the corner of a letter.

'"Towers, 'nkney Road, Hendon,"' Glover read. 'Bit missing from each of the two top lines. Easy to find the complete address, though. Are we going to follow it up?'

'Or ring in first and ask for instructions?'

'Nix on that, mate. It's a rule in this mob that if you do that, you're off the job and put on something a sight worse. 'Least, that's how it always works for me.

'Tell you what,' he went on, 'we'll call in at the local nick. 'Tisn't far from here, and they know me. I was up on some inquiries a short time ago.'

Glover was certainly remembered at Braham Road Police Station. The desk sergeant turned to his clerk as soon as the two young men appeared.

'Have we got an empty cell, Chris? I think we have. That one where all the rats are. Chuck me the keys, will you?'

'Nark it, sarge,' Glover begged. 'We're here for a bit of info. This is Arthur Howard from up north.'

The sergeant grimaced. 'You want to watch it, young man. There isn't a copper in the London area as won't run you in on suspicion if you're seen in Nick Glover's company. What's it all about, anyway?'

Howard showed him the paper and the

sergeant nodded. 'Right. Shouldn't be difficult. Take the desk a minute, Chris, while I look this up.

'That's it,' he said three minutes later. 'Blenheim Towers, Pinkney Road, Hendon. For your further information, it's listed as a private nursing home.'

'Thanks a lot, sarge,' Glover replied. 'I knew we could depend on you. It's like Chief Inspector Amberley said to me when he put me on this job. Any difficulty, Glover, he says, and you go to Braham Road. They'll put you right. And they'll provide transport, seeing this is a rush job and as top secret as they come.'

'Transport?' The sergeant's florid cheeks purpled. 'You cheeky young devil! Transport, he says, when there's a good bus route at the end of the street.'

Glover shrugged. 'Okay, if that's the way, sarge. Only time is of the essence. I'm only just telling you what Chief Inspector Amberley — Hey, who're you ringing?'

'Just going to check with the Yard.' The sergeant looked at Glover as he lifted the telephone. 'I'll be interested to find out, if this is such an urgent, top secret inquiry, why they only put a couple of half-fledged bits of fuzz on it, and failed to provide them with a car.'

'Okay, you win.' Glover grinned disarmingly at him. 'But it was worth a try. End of the street, you said? Right.'

He looked at his watch as they left the station.

'We might just get there and back before lunch. If we're lucky with buses.'

They were. They found Pinkney Road to be one of those wide, quiet London streets which, because they neither come from nor go to anywhere important, carry only a thread of traffic even at the busiest times of the day. Large houses, set well back from the road and faced with lawns, shrubberies and flower borders could be glimpsed beyond ornate iron entrance gates piercing the high brick walls of privacy which almost every house boasted. Blenheim Towers was larger than the average, its drive gates were open and beyond them lay a well-tended lawn graced by a fountain.

A gilt-lettered board on the wall by the

gates proclaimed the nursing home name. Beneath it, in smaller letters, was 'H. Jamieson, M.D., Ch.B.' There was no porter's lodge so the two constables walked briskly up the weedless gravel drive.

'Cost a packet to have a few days here, I'll bet,' Glover commented and added. 'If you like, I'll do the spiel.'

'Suits me, Nick. You know what we're after.'

They mounted a wide flight of steps and found a bell push by the side of a large, nail-studded door. The door opened unexpectedly and a grim, grey-haired woman in nurses' uniform confronted them silently.

'Good morning, nurse. Police.' Glover produced his warrant card slickly. 'We wish to contact a Dr. Lewis Peel and we think we may obtain news of him here.'

She shook her head decisively. 'There is no one of that name in residence.'

'The matter is extremely important,' Glover insisted. 'Perhaps you would be good enough to let Dr. Jamieson know we are here.'

'Dr. Jamieson will not be back until this afternoon. As I cannot help you in any way I suggest you call again later. Not before three-thirty. I will inform the doctor you will be returning then. Good morning.'

The door closed firmly. Glover raised his eyebrows significantly at Howard as they turned away.

11

They passed through the drive gates and halted on the pavement, out of sight of the house.

'Well, what do you propose to do now, Arthur?' Glover asked. 'I mean, it's your case, when all's said and done, so you make the decisions, eh?'

'My orders are to contact Peel as soon as possible, Nick. It looks as if we can only get to him through this Dr. Jamieson, doesn't it?' He brought his wrist up. 'Nearly half-past twelve, and that means three hours before we go up yonder again.'

Glover's face lightened. 'I'll tell you what. You nip off and get a bite to eat. There's a cafe in the main road, opposite where we got off the bus. I'll hang on here till you get back. Then if this Peel should turn up by any chance we can try at the nursing home again.'

'Yes, but how would you recognize

him? I've got no description — they just didn't provide me with one.'

'Dr. Peel, my dear Watson,' Glover returned, 'is a dark-haired man with a long face and heavy eyebrows, a prominent chin and very small ears.'

'No, but kidding apart — '

'No kidding, boy. While you were doing the polite to Mitchell over the snuff-boxes I took a gander at a framed photo on the mantelpiece. Signed 'Lewis.' Okay?'

'Good for you.' Howard hesitated. 'Say, that nurse just now. Didn't she strike you as being a bit too secretive and over-obstructive? Suspicious, I thought.'

'She wasn't what you'd call helpful, certainly. But you know what these places — and the people who staff 'em — are. You get the idea they're trying to cover for all sorts of dirty deeds, but actually it's the old bumptious medical attitude to the layman coming out. Think nothing of it, Arthur. You just buzz off and feed your face.'

'Right, shan't be long.' Howard moved away. There was a telephone box near the end of Pinkney Road. His pace slowed as he neared it. Maybe he ought to ring in and report to somebody, either to Chief Inspector Amberley at the Yard, or to his own H.Q. at Deniston. Spratt's note had told him to 'keep in touch,' but there didn't seem much point in reporting an almost-blank morning. Maybe, after three-thirty, when they'd seen Jamieson . . . Yes, leave it till then. He glanced back before he turned into the main road. Nick Glover was leaning against the wall of the nursing home, hands in pockets. His attitude suggested he was prepared to stay there all day.

The cafe was steamy and crowded. Howard joined the queue at the self-service counter, a long line which seemed to move forward very slowly indeed. But some ten minutes later, when he had unloaded his tray at a table which offered a seat, he dug into his plate contentedly.

But he did not linger over his meal. Fair was fair, and Nick would be wanting his dinner, too. Howard was back at the nursing home soon after one. Judging from his mate's position and posture,

Nick hadn't moved a muscle during the past half-hour.

'Nothing doing,' he said as he heaved himself away from the wall. 'One car only, a dark-blue Cortina driven by a bald man in a wing collar and a black tie. Nobody else with him. He was back inside a quarter of an hour. No Dr. Peel. How was the scoff?'

'Not bad. Bit crowded there, though. You'd better move fast before it's all gone.'

'That I'll do. Oh, I meant to tell you, Arthur. I changed my mind about ringing in — well, I mean, it was something to do, a stroll down to the box yonder — and I let Amberley know where we were and what we were doing. Carry on is the word. See you!'

He waved a hand and went. Howard grinned to himself as he, too, settled against the wall.

He had been long enough in the Deniston C.I.D. to learn the mental boredom and physical weariness of a prolonged spell of uneventful observation. But he began to get fed-up with this job almost before Glover was out of sight. He felt uncomfortable and extremely conspicuous. The road was quiet, with very few pedestrians along the pavement, and there was no convenient doorway nor bus-stop where he could linger for a while without remark. He walked along to the far end of the road, constantly glancing over his shoulder, he returned on the opposite pavement and stopped twice to make a long job of doing up a fictitiously-loose shoelace.

He crossed the road and took stand against the wall again. The afternoon was dull and dry but now it was turning unseasonably cold. From the end of the street he had just left a beat constable appeared, marching slowly but steadily towards him. Howard's instinct was to move along at once, he controlled it with a self-deprecatory shrug. What was he thinking of?

The policeman, who was middle-aged and portly, drew level with him and stopped. Howard felt the Eye run over him.

'Now then, sir,' the constable said. 'You

waiting for somebody?'

'As a matter of fact, I am.' Howard kept his voice low. He felt it would sound better that way. 'Detective Constable Howard, Deniston C.I.D. Down here on a special job.' He produced his warrant card and the man in uniform examined it at arms' length.

'So that's it.' The card was handed back. 'You wouldn't be after a' — quotations marks were clear in his voice — 'fair-haired, vicious-looking young man in a dark brown suit and a fancy waistcoat? Because if you are you've missed him. According to information received by me, he was hanging about here less than ten minutes ago.'

Howard laughed. 'Sounds like a slanderous description of my mate. I've just relieved him to get something to eat. He's from the Yard — Nick Glover.'

'Niver heard of him. Who's he work for?'

'Chief Inspector Amberley — you know, one of Chief Super Browning's team.'

'Right. Well, if I may take the liberty of

advising the Yard and its associates, young man, let me suggest you don't stand around looking like a coupla thugs to folks who live in these houses opposite. Which, as a result, I get notified by a householder about persons acting suspicious and have to detour from me normal beat, and waste time, seeing I'll have to contact the said householder again, which to my mind, isn't . . . ' Having got himself thoroughly entangled in his sentence, he cut his losses. 'So do me a favour and watch it, will-ya?'

'Sure, sure.' Howard wished him good-day hurriedly and turned quickly. While they had been talking he had faced the main road and he had been conscious of brisk footsteps approaching from behind, but these had now ceased, though Howard thought he could catch the crunch of trodden gravel. He walked past the drive gates.

A man in a light-weight, dark blue overcoat and a black trilby was going up the drive. Under the brim of the hat Howard could see a plentiful crop of dark hair and a pair of smallish ears. He put the man's height at around six feet. It could be Peel, according to Glover's description, though Howard had no opportunity to note the other items, the heavy eyebrows and the firm protuberant chin.

He paused irresolutely. Dash after the fellow and ask him who he was? And then, if it wasn't Peel, drop in for a heap of confusing explanations? Better let it ride. He turned back again and now he saw the man swing away from the entrance steps to take a path which led round the house. Risking possible observation from the nursing home windows, Howard stepped inside the gates, on to a grass border which separated a narrow shrubbery from the drive. From here he saw a side door, and the man had halted in front of it, his hand raised in the act of knocking. A brief pause, and he was admitted.

In the act of moving back into the road, Howard noticed the shrubbery. It was narrow, but thick, with wide-spreading rhododendrons and laurels. It ran, on his left, along two sides of the wall and then made a second right-angle to project some distance towards the house walls. Where it ended, Howard saw a greenhouse, with a trellised arch beside it leading, obviously, to the back garden. He also noticed the space, almost pathlike, which ran behind the shrubs underneath the wall.

He stepped quickly into this space and, at once, into concealment. Here was the best observation post of all — if he hadn't been spotted diving for it. If he had, and someone came down from the house to see what he was about, he could go all official on them. At anyrate, it was a pleasant shelter from the nip of the wind.

He walked along the foot of the wall until he reached the corner where it turned away from the road. Another glance at his watch assured him that Glover wasn't likely to be back yet. Still hidden from view from all but the attic windows of the nursing home, he went on.

This was the party wall which divided the home from its neighbouring house. The path was still wide enough to make easy travelling for an active young man. At the next corner the shrubs were backed by interwoven overlap fencing in six feet high panels. A few more yards and he was looking into the greenhouse, packed with plants on a double staging. No signs of human occupation showed inside it. He edged his way to its corner, clear of the shrubbery now. There was the door the visitor had entered and standing at gaze out of a large window on the left of it was the visitor himself. Howard retreated at once. Confident the man had not been looking in his direction, he disappeared quickly but warily. He took with him a glimpse of thick dark hair, a long face and a boot-like chin.

He crept to the edge of the shrubbery, parted branches and looked again. The hair, the ears, the chin were as Peel had been described to him and — yes, now he saw the heavy eyebrows.

The head at the window turned sharply, as if someone had come into the room there. The man picked up his hat, swung quickly round and disappeared from Howard's view. Time to do a disappearing act myself, Howard thought, and was moving back to the rear of the shrubbery when an elderly man in a gardener's apron came through the trellised arch and walked slowly round towards the front of the house.

Howard gave the man ample time to get out of the way before he himself began to retrace his way along the foot of the wall. As he reached the side which bordered the street he heard a car's door close and the sound of an engine. He was half-way along the wall when a black Bentley swept down the drive and through the gates. The man he had seen at the house window was sitting in solitary state in the rear, the car driver was a swarthy young man in chauffeur's uniform.

Howard sprinted the last few yards and made a flying leap into the roadway, almost into the arms of Nick Glover.

'And where,' the Yard man demanded, 'd'you think you've been?'

Howard told his tale quickly and Glover's eyes showed his interest.

'It could have been Peel from what you

say,' he agreed. 'I didn't get much of a look at him myself, actually my eye was taken by something in the car.'

'I wish I could have got a word with him,' Howard said. 'I mean, I was unlucky not to stop him when he went in. If it hadn't been for that beat man . . . '

He told his friend the story. Glover laughed and clapped him on the shoulder.

'Cheer up, mate. I gotta proposition. We'll follow him and accost him at his destination.' He saw the puzzled look on Howard's face and let it remain there a moment or two. 'I said I noticed something in the car — on the front seat by the driver. A very handsome, very expensive wreath.'

'So what?'

'The car turned right-handed, into Brent Street. Headed for Golders Green, I'll bet a penny. And even you backwoods boys will know what takes blokes with wreaths to Golders Green.'

'You think he's headed for a funeral?'

'I do. So let us hie, as they say, yonder there ourselves. It isn't far. About a mile.

And there's always a bus.'

'And supposing you're wrong? Or suppose the chap isn't Peel? We can't go bullocking into a private funeral.'

'Look, Arthur. We can't see this Dr. Jamieson before half past three. Twenty past two now. We've loads of time to spare and we might as well take a bus ride — or I'm game to walk it if you like — as hang about here and be subjected to insults from the flippin' local populace, backed by clever-devil coppers on beat.'

'You win, Nick. Let's go.'

They just missed a bus and, rather than wait in the cold for another, they used their legs. They crossed North Circular Road and made good time along Golders Green Road and so to the best-known crematorium in Britain. Funeral traffic, coming and going, made the place as busy as an international airport.

'One black Bentley's going to take a bit of finding amongst this lot,' Howard said. 'I didn't get the number, either, did you?'

'No, but not to worry, boy. Look over there. That's her.'

The Bentley was drawn up in a

semi-circular bay off the main path. The swarthy-skinned chauffeur stood leaning against the bonnet, idly watching the ebb and flow of vehicles and people. The detectives crossed to him and Glover spoke.

'You're from Blenheim Towers Nursing Home, aren't you?'

The chauffeur stared a moment, then smiled with a flash of white teeth.

'Si — that is, yais. Some business of yoursa, is it, that where I come from?'

Glover ignored the question to ask another. 'Who was the gentleman you brought here today?'

The chauffeur stared again, but this time he did not smile. Nor did he reply.

'Look,' Glover said, and fished out his wallet. 'We're police officers, on an inquiry. You're Italian, aren't you?'

'Si. Police? You wanta see papers from me?'

'We just want to know the name of the man you brought here.'

'I don' know, signor. All I know I am told to get the car out and breeng zis man here.'

'Was his name Peel, Dr. Peel?'

'Pill? I say to you, I don' know. It is true.'

'Right. Where has he gone?'

'Somewhere. He don' tella me. All he say is to get the car outa the way and wait. This I do.'

'There was a wreath on the front seat when you left the nursing home. Did he take it with him? Did he go inside?'

The chauffeur nodded vigorously at both questions.

'I move the car, like he say. I am in the way of a' — he pointed to a hearse which had just drawn up — 'one of them. I back and make the turn. I see the signor go in behind a — a death box with the flowers. Is all.'

'Well, thanks. We want a word with this gentleman, so we'll wait, also, till he comes back.'

The Italian nodded, and, apparently dismissing them from his mind, resumed his observation of life — and death.

Howard and Glover withdrew some distance. 'So your guess was right, Nick,' the Deniston man said. 'He came here to attend a funeral.'

'Yeah. These crematorium jobs are soon over so we shouldn't have long to wait. And, whether it's Peel or not, we should be able to win a ride back to the nursing home. The car's almost sure to be returning there. Popular job nowadays, this cremating, ain't it?'

They discussed the pros and cons of cremation and earth burial, and went on to argue as to the most comfortable way of committing suicide. Glover was becoming eloquent on the advantages of slashing the wrists while reclining in a hot bath when they saw the Italian spring into alertness as the man he had driven to the Green came out from beneath an archway and walked towards the car.

'I'll leave the chat to you this time,' Glover murmured as they, too, went forward. 'And if it isn't your man, I'll back you up in humblest apologies.'

The chauffeur was opening the rear door of the car.

'Excuse me, sir.' Howard stepped to the passenger's side. 'Are you Dr. Lewis Peel of the University of Deniston?'

The man swung round. Grey eyes, hardening suddenly, stared at Howard levelly.

'Why do you ask? Who are you? If you're the Press — '

'Police officers, sir. I am from Deniston, my colleague is from Scotland Yard. You *are* Dr. Peel?'

'Of course. Well?'

'The safe in your office at the university has been broken into, sir, and papers of yours, thought to be of importance and secrecy' — Howard was quoting from Sergeant Spratt's note — 'are missing. We weren't able to get in touch with you — er — through normal channels, I was sent to London, we've seen Mr. Charles Mitchell and so ... That's why we're here, sir.'

Peel frowned. 'I don't understand how you traced me. But I fear you have had your journey to no purpose, officer. Those papers of mine were not of importance.' He made a move to enter the car.

'I'd like a detailed statement, sir,' Howard insisted. 'You see, a crime has been committed and the police have a job to do. If you could give me particulars of what was in the safe, sir . . . '

'Of course. Perhaps we could talk in the car. I think I am ready — No, wait a moment! I've forgotten to — Look here, I shan't be a couple of seconds!'

He strode away from them, towards the archway from which he had come. He did not seem to be in any particular hurry and Howard, hesitating as to whether he should accompany Peel, looked at Glover, whose dubious expression gave him no help.

Ten long minutes later they went in search of Dr. Lewis Peel, in different directions and after strict injunctions to the chauffeur not to leave, with or without his passenger. But nobody to whom they spoke, officials, clergy, undertakers or mourners, could give them any help at all. The scientist had vanished.

'We ought to have gone with him, Arthur,' Glover mourned, and Howard was grateful for the 'we.' 'But he seemed to be acting straight enough, and, I mean, there was the car he was supposed to go back in. I never dreamt for one moment he'd pull such a fast one.'

'It's turned three-thirty now,' Howard said. They were standing once again by the car with their hopes at zero. 'We should be getting back to Blenheim Towers.'

They put this to the chauffeur, who shrugged. He was at as great a loss as they were. To remain, or to go, he could not know how to do, he explained.

'He's skipped, no doubt of it,' Howard decided. 'Let's get back there.' And, after several minutes of forceful argument, backed by the waving of warrant cards, the chauffeur was persuaded to take them.

At Blenheim Towers they found everything except a red carpet and a small girl with a bouquet, laid on for them. The nurse they had previously seen answered the door, she beamed upon them and said Dr. Jamieson would see them at once. She conducted them to a handsomely-furnished study, where a stout, bald man with a round pleasant face rose from behind a large desk to greet them, pressing a bell-stud on the desk as he did so.

'Gentlemen! You've come here to look for Dr. Peel. He has been here, and has gone again. I have to give you his most sincere apologies.'

Howard had had enough of polite methods. 'That's not good enough, sir! Dr. Peel knew we were police officers who wished to question him. He'd no right — '

'Now, just take it easy, laddie.' The doctor's Scottish accent became more pronounced. 'I've rung for tea, so ye'll just sit yourselves down and have a wee cup while I explain.'

'Thanks, but we've no time — '

'Ye'll have time, surely, to listen to what I have to say.' He broke off as a smart maidservant entered with a loaded tray. 'Thanks, Sheena, put it on the desk. That'll be all.' He waited until the maid had gone. 'Now, then. You told Dr. Peel that certain papers had been taken from his safe at the university. Because of this, he has had to go to the Ministry to report the theft and to receive further instructions from them.'

'But he said the papers were valueless!'

Howard burst out.

Dr. Jamieson spread his hands. 'I'm to tell you from him that this may prove to be a matter which officialdom would prefer not to be handled in the ordinary way by the police. That is why he thought it wisest to — shall we say, sidestep you for the moment? If it is decided that Scotland Yard, or the Deniston police force, shall go ahead in this matter, they will be informed at once. So, you see, it's out of your hands and you'll now content yourselves and let me pour out tea.'

Glover nodded. 'Fair enough, doctor. I know how awkward these Special Branch bods can be. But I'd feel easier with some backing from my chief. Could I telephone from here?'

Jamieson gestured at his desk instrument. 'Use this. Our domestic switchboard will put you through.'

At the other end of the line, Chief Inspector Amberley was concise and brief.

'Right,' he said when he had listened to Glover's outline report. 'Drop it, and get back here as quick as you can.' But Nick

Glover translated those orders as permission to stay at Blenheim Towers long enough to drink two cups of tea and to sample some excellent shortbread.

'Dr. Peel is a friend of yours, I take it, sir?' Howard ventured as he stirred sugar into his cup.

Jamieson shook his head. 'An acquaintance only. Look, to save you further probing, I'll explain. It's very simple. Dr. Peel had a friend here in my care. A difficult case, where cure was impossible and deterioration inevitable. The patient died and was cremated this afternoon. As Dr. Peel was in London he wished to attend the funeral. The body was taken from here direct to the undertaker's Chapel of Rest. Dr. Peel was the only mourner, an engagement having prevented me from joining him.'

Howard said, 'I see.' It all sounded reasonable enough, even if it had come out a little too slickly. 'Have you had this patient in residence long, sir?'

Jamieson smiled in gentle reproof. 'One does not discuss one's patients to persons not relatives, even to police officers, you know. Take another piece of shortbread.'

'All the same,' Glover argued when they left the house, 'it's very odd to me, the way Peel seems not to want his wife to know just what he's doing. Didn't you say he told her he had to go to a conference?'

Howard nodded, but did not pursue possibilities. The job was getting too complicated for him.

At the Yard, Chief Inspector Amberley heard their story and told them bleakly they could hardly congratulate themselves. They had had their man and had let him get away. Ministry business or no, that was a sin a policeman should never commit, and well they must know it.

'And now,' he ended, 'you'd better get hold of a line and report to your own people, Howard.'

In Deniston, Spratt took Howard's call. He listened, grunting sardonically at intervals. 'Okay,' he said, 'let's have you back here, then.'

'Tonight, sarge? I mean, I've got a room booked.'

Spratt told him to hang on while he had a word with Mr. Hallam. Then, 'First thing in the morning, remember,' His voice growled.

Nick Glover was delighted. He was free that evening himself.

'So we go up west together,' he said, and Howard did not argue about that.

12

Hallam and Spratt, on that Wednesday morning after their interview with Gerald Dickson, made good time across the city to Patrick Molloy's lodgings in Jackman Street. The Ford Popular was standing outside, the door was opened to them by a plump woman with blue-rinsed grey hair, who announced herself as Mrs. Crosby when Hallam asked her name. She looked doubtful at learning their errand.

'Nay,' she said. 'Patrick's asleep — he works nights, you know. I hardly like to wake him up. Wouldn't it do later on?'

'I'm afraid not, Mrs. Crosby. The matter is very urgent.'

'Well, I suppose you'd better come in.' She showed them into the room they had used on their previous visit, and, hesitating at the door, asked, 'Is it about this business at the university, then? I thought you talked to Pat about that yesterday?'

'Just tell Mr. Molloy we want him to help us a little more, Mrs. Crosby. I'm sure he'll be ready to co-operate.'

Molloy, unshaven, in a worn dressing-gown and slippers, was yawning and rubbing his eyes when he came into the room. But there was a spring-like tension about him which made Hallam suspect he wasn't as sleepy as he wished them to believe.

'Sure, an' this is a foine time to be disturbing a man,' he grumbled. 'And what is it now? Has the ould place burned to the ground entoirely?'

'We're sorry to have roused you, Mr. Molloy,' Hallam said pleasantly. 'But it was necessary. I suppose you heard of the second bit of trouble up there last night?'

'Ah, they were talking about a safe in Science having been bust open. But that's not on my rounds at all, ye know. So I can't be telling you anything about it.'

Hallam spread his hands. 'We had to make sure, of course. There's just one other thing, but that's going back to the night before, when Mr. Bradley was killed. We have a report that some students were climbing the clock tower that night. Did you see them?'

'Never hide nor hair of 'em, sir. I don't get around that way, as I've just been after telling you.'

'I think you know one of them, though. Name of Dickson, Gerald Dickson.'

Molloy had been standing with his hands in his pockets. He now took out a packet of cigarettes, extracted one, tapped it on a thumb-nail and put it in his mouth.

'Dickson?' he repeated. 'Let's see, now. Would he have red hair and a sort of scrubby beard?'

'That describes him fairly accurately.'

'Then I do know the lad. I admit so.'

'And how did you happen to make his acquaintance, Mr. Molloy? I would have thought you night-guards didn't see much of the students, in the normal way.'

Molloy stepped across to the mantel-piece to pick up a matchbox which lay there, though he did not attempt to light his cigarette.

'Och, it was just chance. There's late dances and that at the Union place up yonder, you know, and we happened to get to chatting one night when he came out of there and we met be chance, you see.' He took out a match at last and lit his cigarette.

'We had to see these climbers,' Hallam went on, 'and Dickson proved to be one of them. There was a possibility they could have been of help in the matter of Mr. Bradley's death. But no luck there. I take it you haven't thought of anything more connected with that evening?' Molloy shook his head. 'In that case we'll let you return to bed, Mr. Molloy. Yes, sergeant? Something to say?'

'Well, not really, sir. I was just thinking what a coincidence it was, Detective Constable Howard seeing Mr. Molloy in his car down Willow Street way yesterday afternoon, and Dickson working in Price's garage there. But you haven't read Howard's report, have you, sir?'

'No. What's this all about?' Hallam looked duly mystified.

'You know that other job we sent Howard on?'

'Ah, yes! Of course! I remember.' He

turned to Molloy again, smiling. 'You were at Willow Street yesterday, then?'

Molloy coughed on a lungful of smoke. 'Me? You mean at some garage or other? Now, why would I be doing that, and me car outside there, if it's old, as good as ever? Sure, it wasn't a bad day at all and I thought I'd enjoy a bit of a run round. Likely I was that way you're talking about, but I wouldn't be checking on all the streets I used.'

'Of course not.' Hallam made a move towards the door. 'We mustn't keep you any longer from your rest.'

They took their leave, and as their car moved off Spratt said, 'Shook him, didn't it, sir, the bit about Willow Street? I reckon he won't get off to sleep again very soon. He was worried about that.'

'He certainly told us a different story from the one Dickson gave us. Which was, of course, the object of our exercise. This turn on the left, take it — quick!'

Spratt made a sharp fourth-to-second gear change and just managed to pull the car round into the narrow side street his chief inspector had indicated.

'Dickson,' Hallam explained. 'He's just turned into Jackman Street, and coming this way. No mistaking him. Probably came by bus. We'll check on him.'

Spratt found a second left-hand turning and drove into it. He stopped the car and got out, strolling casually back into the first side street they had taken, where he halted in front of a small general shop to gaze interestedly at the tired-looking stock in its tiny window. He saw Dickson hurry past the street end without looking to left or right. Spratt moved on to the corner from which he could see along Jackman Street; there was a convenient pillar-box there behind which he stopped. But Dickson, obviously on an urgent errand, was not glancing behind him. He turned in at Patrick Molloy's lodgings, took an envelope from his breast pocket, thrust it through the letter-box and at once turned away. Spratt went quickly back to the police car, confident he had not been seen.

'So,' Hallam commented when he had heard the story, 'our red-haired friend was anxious that Molloy's tale should check with his own, if we got around to talking to Molloy. He knew the guard would likely have gone to bed at this time, so he left a note. I'd give a great deal to know what goes on between those two. But I think, at the moment, we'll continue to let them have rope. Drive us to Willow Street, Jack. We'll have a word with Evan Price next.'

They found the proprietor alone in the garage making up accounts in the tiny office. He was not at all perturbed at seeing Hallam and Spratt, both of whom he knew.

'One of your chaps was here yesterday,' he said. 'Didn't say who he was, see? If he had I'd have given him every assist-ance. You know that, Mr. Hallam. And I wouldn't have let my boys play up with him, whatever.'

'I'm sure you wouldn't.' Hallam didn't get the hang of the playing-up remark but he let it ride. 'At any rate, you assisted our man to get the information he needed. We're here for a little more of the same thing.'

'Anything I can do, Mr. Hallam, now.'

'There's just one point. We can't make you give answers to our questions, as you well know, but those questions will be in confidence, as your answers will be if you give them. I hope that's quite clear?'

'Clear and fair it is, now.'

'Bear in mind, Mr. Price, about the confidential questions. You see, if you don't repeat them to anybody until a certain case at the university here is cleared up, if you keep them entirely to yourself, there may come a time — who knows? — when we'll be glad to show our gratitude.'

Price's eyes opened widely. 'I don't know why you should say that at all! Don't get it, I don't.'

'Leave it, then. Now, to start with, do you know a man called Patrick Molloy?'

The Welshman's reply was instantaneous. 'No.'

'Irish, as you can guess,' Hallam persisted. 'Tall, well-made, thirtyish, good-looking. Dark hair and blue eyes. He may have called here for a minor repair job. Drives an old Ford Popular.'

Price shook his head decisively. 'Still

don't ring any bells.'

'Right. You have a couple of university students who come to work here, I understand.'

Price was frowning now. 'Yes, but are you going to tell me I shouldn't employ them? Was there some regulation? Look, now, I let these boys do jobs to help me out, and I pay them as casual workers, see? What's the harm?'

'None at all. We just want your opinion about them. As I said before, in strict confidence. Let's take Brian Markham, for instance.'

'He hasn't been coming here long, Mr. Hallam. His pal Dickson brought him. But he's a good mechanic, knows engines nearly as well as I do, now. Qui-et lad, he is. Hasn't much to say for himself.'

'He told me he was cursed with a quick temper.'

'Never seen a sign of it here, I haven't. De-vo-ted, I would say, to engines, see. Don't get mad even if a job goes wrong. Sort of coaxes it right, like as if a car engine was alive.'

'And he's honest? I mean, he wouldn't

pocket a tool, or any money lying about?'

'Honest as the day, he is.'

'Good. Now Dickson, his pal. How did he get going here in the first place?'

Price laughed. 'Ginger Dickson! I've known him ever since I opened up here and that's over ten years ago. He was always hanging around when he was a nipper. Felt sorry for him, I did, gave him many a penny to spend.'

'His home was around here, then?'

'If you could call it a home. He was at the orphanage yonder, beyond the railway bridge.'

'He's done pretty well for himself, hasn't he? An orphanage boy, now a university student?'

'Ah, he has brains, you see. And his teachers, they helped him. Brains he has, and bounce with them. It always was like that with Ginger.'

'Ginger,' Spratt repeated. 'Yes, of course, it does fit him. Though I believe he gets called 'Red' at the university.'

Price grinned. 'And that's not only because of his hair, look you. He's a big member of the university communist party, or society, whatever they call it. Hot he is, on this communism, very hot. Talk a man to death about it he would, now.'

'You're not a sympathiser yourself, it seems, Mr. Price?'

'Me? It's a load of old rubbish they preach, Mr. Hallam. But they're young, see? Young and big-headed. Same as us at that age, know everything what's best for other people. They'll grow out of it, look, like we did, but I wish Ginger would buck up about it. Fed-up, I am, hearing all this about Red China.'

'Oh, one of those, is he? Not a Russian red?'

'Indeed no. Got no use for the Kremlin, he says. Let world communism down bad, them chaps have. But he's harmless, when all's said and done, is Ginger.'

Three minutes later they were back in the car, and Hallam knew they had left a very mystified Welshman behind them. Price would be trying to puzzle out just why they had asked those questions.

'Does that mean we've got a line at last, sir?' Spratt asked eagerly. 'A young

Commie, and top-secret papers lifted from Peel's safe? His work was to do with new alloys, you know, which spells space-travel stuff to me. And the Chinese are trying hard to get into that.'

'We'll wait until we can get hold of Peel,' Hallam replied, 'before we theorize further. However, we haven't wasted our morning. We've proved Dickson's story a tissue of lies from start to finish. A spot of lunch now, and then we'll go over the whole of this case once again. And keep your fingers crossed!'

13

Gerald Dickson, returning to Monkbridge House, took the lift to the fourth floor. He had reached the door of his room when his next-door neighbour put out his head.

'Thought I recognized the fairy feet. Here, some bloke's been trying to get you on the blower, Red. I took a message — would you ring Mr. Smith as soon as you came in. Said it was urgent.'

'Thanks, Tony. Will do.' Dickson went into his room. His books and papers lay as he had left them when, after the two policemen had gone, he realized he'd better get in touch with Pat Molloy straight away, just in case it occurred to the cops to do a bit of checking up. He hoped Molloy would get the note he had written in good time; maybe he should have insisted on seeing the Irishman, but that would have meant waking him up, and a lot of explanations to his landlady.

He stood for several minutes staring

sightlessly out of the window, a prey to worry and foreboding. As it had turned out, he'd been a fool to get himself into all this. They'd told him his part would be simple enough, and the pay he had drawn was generous, but things hadn't gone the way they'd been planned.

He glanced at his watch, shrugged, and went out to the telephone in the corridor. His finger dialled a number he now knew by heart, and at the fourth ring he was answered, by a high-pitched, impatient-sounding voice.

'Smith here, who is it?'

'Gerald Dickson. I got a message to call you.'

'Yes. Listen carefully. You will meet our mutual friend this evening, at seven o'clock precisely. Same place where you met yesterday afternoon. That is clear?'

'Yes, but — Look, I've got to pull out of this. You know very well I'd never have had anything to do with it all if I'd thought — '

'You're wasting your time, Dickson. Also mine.'

'But the police have been here to see

me this morning. They know I met — '

'No names.' The command came hissing over the wire. 'Just don't worry, that's all. And keep the appointment this evening.' The telephone went dead.

Dickson stood for some moments, the receiver still in his hand, his lips a tight line, his red eyebrows drawn. Then he laid the receiver down and took out a pocket diary. He turned to a page, memorized a number on it, picked up the telephone again and dialled.

'Brampton's Superstores,' a woman's voice answered crisply.

'Er — could I possibly speak to Miss Janice Kilburn, please?'

'Is it important? I think she's in the storeroom and, you see — well, I can't leave my switchboard. Would you like to give me a message?'

'I'd rather speak to her personally. And it is urgent — really.'

'Hold on, then. I'll see what I can do.' And, after an interval, another girl's voice, almost breathless.

'Janice Kilburn here.'

Dickson spoke quickly. 'It's Gerry,

Janice. Look, I know I shouldn't be ringing you in business hours, but I just had to get hold of you. Can you meet me on the waste bit of ground behind the garage tonight, just before seven? Please!'

'Oh, I don't know, I'm sure. I'd half-promised to go out with Shirley tonight. Anyway, we don't shut here till six. I couldn't possibly get home, have a meal and get ready by that time.'

Dickson's fist beat a tattoo against the wall.

'Listen, Jan. You've got to be there by seven. Please, don't let me down. This is desperately urgent. Please, Jan!'

'All right, then.' A laugh came pleasantly. 'Seeing it's you. But no more ringing me at work, remember. Promise?'

Dickson gave his word, returned to his room, unearthed a packet of biscuits from a locker and sat down at the desk in the window. He took out a pen and bent to the work he had left that morning, chewing away, without relish, at the biscuits which were a substitute for his normal lunch. But he was soon leaning back, frowning and biting his lower lip.

He couldn't concentrate, he had too much on his mind to allow for the scientific calculations in front of him. And as he gazed at the mental picture his brain conjured up, fear began to take the place of mere worry. Fear which made his heart pound and sweat to bead his forehead. Suddenly, like a trapped animal flinging itself against the bars of the cage into which it has been lured, he sprang up, sending his chair flying.

He rushed downstairs and hurried to the University Union. Two quick drinks at the bar failed to lighten his apprehension. And then it was time for his afternoon lectures.

Mercifully, both were theoretical. No lab work today. He'd have cut that, anyway. In the state he was in he could no more have handled delicate apparatus than an armless man could deal a hand of cards. In a back corner of the lecture room he sat withdrawn, scribbling now and then in his notebook just for the look of the thing. He wrote automatically, as random thoughts, sudden ideas, came up from the seething whirlpool of his brain.

When, at the end of the first lecture, he stood up with the others, he looked at what he had put down.

'Inform police? . . . B. Markham might be persuaded . . . Or Taff, if I threaten exposure . . . Tell Janice all?'

He tore the pages from his notebook, ripped them across and across into tiny pieces and dropped them into the lecture room wastepaper basket on his way out. A silly habit, putting thoughts on paper, even half-formed, indecisive thoughts. Could be incriminating.

The second lecture dragged on interminably. Even when it was over, the time was only half-past four. Two and a half hours more and then, come what might, he'd get this job settled as far as he was concerned, or know the reason why!

He caught a bus to Albert Road, next to Willow Street, quite twenty minutes earlier than he need have done. He was annoyed with himself for doing so, recognizing it as a sign of extreme nervousness, yet knowing himself incapable of resisting it. But he wouldn't turn up at the appointed place a moment before he need. He promised himself that. It meant, when the bus put him down at the end of Albert Road, that he had time to kill. His girl friend, Janice Kilburn, lived within a hundred yards of Albert Road, and he was tempted to go there first. But if he did he wouldn't be a welcome visitor, with Janice upstairs rushing around to get ready to meet him, and her mother and father secretly annoyed at being disturbed when they had settled to watch evening television. So he roamed the streets in the vicinity and looked repeatedly at his watch. The light drizzle which had set in showed no signs of clearing, but Dickson hardly noticed it.

And then at last it really was time to make his way to the piece of waste ground, to meet Janice — and the man whom Patrick Molloy, who was always present at such conferences, would have brought across in his old car before he went to his night's work at the university. But, when Dickson turned off the pavement of Albert Road, on to the empty area, there was no Ford Popular lurking in the shadows of the surrounding houses. Just a small van — looked like an Austin Countryman — parked facing towards the road, round a corner where a passing constable, aware of the No Parking notice, was not likely to see it.

Dickson was walking past the van, wondering if Pat had chosen a new spot to park in, when the vehicle's engine started up, roaring under a depressed accelerator-pedal. A man stepped out from the far side of the van into Dickson's path. The young student never saw the gun which pumped two quick shots into his body. He fell like a poleaxed beast.

His killer bent over him for a few moments, then sprang into the already-moving van. It bumped its way on to Albert Road, picked up speed swiftly, and was gone.

★ ★ ★

Janice Kilburn had known Gerald Dickson from his orphanage days. Her father was gardener and general handyman at that grim institution — he still held the post — and as a tiny girl she had often toddled along with him there. 'Ginger' Dickson, nearly three years older than herself, had been her childhood hero. There was nothing Ginger was too scared to try, and, in his view, rules and regulations were only there to break.

They had lost touch, of course, when Ginger went to the grammar school; Janice had never been any sort of a bet for the Eleven Plus examination. She had been flattered, therefore, when Ginger had looked her up in his first university year and had seemed quite keen to renew the old friendship. She had been his partner at several university dances and they had done a few shows together. Janice could never make up her mind whether she really considered him as her 'steady.' She wasn't in love with him, and he had certainly showed no signs of being passionately devoted to her. Just good pals, who'd do anything for each other, but no strings attached, no deep involvements. She was going to meet him now

— with a plastic hood over her shining fair hair against the drizzle — after a snatched meal, but only because he had sounded so desperately insistent on the phone. She'd no idea what it was all about, but, for the sake of old times, she'd been forced to say yes.

She turned in at the empty space between the houses in Albert Road and began to walk across it. She had met Ginger here several times after he had finished a spell of work at the garage. He didn't seem to be about just now, though. The waste ground was overshadowed by its surrounding houses, there were pools of duskiness here and there but still it was light enough to see even a stationary figure.

At first glance, she thought the crumpled object on the ground was a sack of old rubbish someone had dumped there. It lay in a hollow and she had almost stumbled over it. And then it moved, and groaned, the head twisted and Janice saw. There was no mistaking the flaming hair, the scrubby beard which she had never been able to persuade him to give up. She uttered one startled cry, then dropped to her knees beside him. But even as she tried to cradle the head into some comfort, it fell sideways on a slackened neck and his body went limp in her arms.

She pushed her hand inside the jacket he wore, in an attempt to feel his heart. But she jerked her fingers quickly back again and thrust them upwards into the light. This time she screamed, springing to her feet and wiping those fingers convulsively on her coat. Then she turned and ran, towards the telephone box at the corner of the waste ground. The fingers she forced to dial three nines were still stained redly. She gasped out her message before she crumpled to the floor of the box in a merciful faint.

★ ★ ★

Chief Inspector Hallam was at home, in slippered comfort, with a good meal inside him and his pipe and the evening paper all ready to hand. But he neither lit the one nor opened the other. He sat staring into the fire. For once he was breaking his own rule not to take the office home with him.

His wife leaned across from her own chair and laid a hand on his knee.

'Trouble?' she asked gently. 'Come on, Bill, out with it. Bottling it up will do you no good at all.'

He moved restlessly. 'It's this confounded university case — or cases, Kathie. There's no starting point. Jack Spratt and I spent the whole afternoon pulling the job to pieces and trying to put it together again to make some sort of sense. We might as well have gone to the pictures!'

He snatched up his pipe and began to cram tobacco into it. His wife said nothing. She knew the signs. For once, Bill was bursting to talk it out, all over again and this time in the presence of an unofficial, sympathetic listener. She was more than willing to accept the role.

'We're practically certain, you see, Kathie, that this chap Bradley had an appointment to meet the man who's still lying unconscious at St. Mary's, because it must be Humpkin in that hospital. Since the science department safe was cleared out the same night — that is, if Dr. Peel himself didn't empty it — it's feasible to believe Bradley was killed because he saw something or somebody he wasn't meant to see, connected with the safe job. But we can't work on that until we know definitely about Peel. Young Howard found him in London, and let him get away again. The story Peel left for his doctor friend at the nursing home to tell is phony from start to finish, in my opinion. Jack doesn't seem to be so sure on that point.'

Kathie Hallam nodded encouragingly. She had no idea at all what Bill was talking about when he brought in a Dr. Peel and a nursing home. There had been nothing in the papers about it. But Bill was now so engrossed in his problems that he had overlooked the fact she was ignorant on such details, and she wasn't going to interrupt the flow of his thoughts by pointing this out to him. So she merely nodded.

'There seems to be some sort of a

tie-up between one of the students and a night security guard. Both of them were on the university premises when the two crimes took place. The guard had every right to be there, of course, and the student seemed to be fully occupied in trying to climb the clock tower. It doesn't seem likely he even knew of the existence of Bradley, the archivist. And the two students who might have had it in for Bradley are clear, as far as we can prove. It's that confounded Dr. Peel who's the nigger in the woodpile. He once quarrelled with Bradley, it was his safe which was cleared, he dashed off to London and gave his wife a lying reason for doing so, and he seems to have been appearing and disappearing down there like a billiard ball in the hand of a conjuror. Apparently he attended a funeral this afternoon, but whether this was merely incidental to his chief purpose, or not, can't be decided yet. Of course, I should have had more sense than to send a raw detective constable after him. But it seemed a simple errand at the time I made the decision.'

'Yes, dear.'

'And, worst of all, there's a distinct smell of Official Secrets Act about this Peel disappearance. I had Browning of the Yard on the phone just before I left the office. He's been dropping some questions here and there, just casually, like, and it seems Peel is one of the really big scientific bugs, though he gets very little publicity for most of the government work he does. There's always the chance of side-changing with these chaps, and that's what's scaring me. Though, somehow, I don't see Peel doing it. I've been in his house, you know, and I've met his wife. You can get a fair idea of how a marriage is going, can't you, from the atmosphere of a home, even if you meet only one of the partners. Or am I being too fanciful there, Kathie?'

'I wouldn't say so, Bill. I'd trust your judgement.'

'Thanks. Jack Spratt had the same impression about the Peels. It's a new house, you know, and they haven't been married very long. We did some digging into Peel's background this afternoon. We both had the feeling, at his house, that there was a definite permanency being built up there — a sort of — oh, a planned future is the best way I can express it. So we took another run up to the university when Howard's report came in. We had a talk with the bursar there. Peel, he told us, could have had jobs all over the country, and in America, for the asking — he's as eminent as that. But he's made it very clear, and very definite, he intends to stay in Deniston. His wife is a local girl and they've lots of friends here. Which all seems to underline that home impression I talked about. But none of it helps us with Bradley's murder, which is my main headache. Frankly, I just don't know what to do next.'

His wife smiled. 'You might light that pipe, for a start. You haven't done so yet.'

'Haven't I? Good lord, and I've been sucking at it hard enough.'

He spoke next out of a blue cloud. 'That's better. Oh, and there's another vague sort of point. The student, Dickson, who is known as 'Red,' seems to be quite a Commie. Of course, you do get

234

lots of those among students, and they don't mean any harm, usually. They grow out of it, too. Dickson was brought up in an orphanage, it's quite possible that gave him a chip on his shoulder.'

Kathie Hallam murmured, 'Quite likely,' content to see that Bill was relaxing at last, that this spell of talking had done him good. He smiled at her.

'Ah, well, my dear, tomorrow is another day. So we'll leave it.'

He picked up the paper, scanned the front-page headlines and turned to the sports section. The telephone in the hall began to ring.

'I'll get it.' Kathie was on her feet at once. She saw the look in her husband's eyes and added, 'It's probably only Florence. She said she'd get in touch with me about that sale of work.'

But Hallam let the newspaper fall. He had a foreboding. Kathie had not closed the door behind her and her voice came clearly.

'Yes, he is, but he's really only just got home . . . Yes . . . Yes, of course, sergeant. I'll get him for you.'

Hallam was already at the door. Kathie, her hand over the telephone's mouthpiece, shrugged helplessly.

'Something very urgent, dear. They wouldn't be put off.' She sighed. 'Who'd be a policeman's wife?'

'Who'd be a policeman?' Hallam echoed as he took the receiver from her.

He listened, saying only, 'Yes,' or, 'I see,' while Kathie hovered in the background. Then, 'Right. I'll get along there at once. I'll need Sergeant Spratt — lay on transport for him, will you? Oh, and, Joe, this will be a full-scale inquiry so I want everyone alerted, besides the on-duty men. Can you get that going? I'll take full responsibility if there are any questions or snags. Got that? Good.'

He cradled the telephone and stood looking at his wife, his eyes withdrawn and absent. Suddenly, he grinned, without mirth.

'So everything happens to me! And this'll be an all-night job if I'm not very, very lucky. Kathie, it's the damnedest thing. That student Dickson has been shot dead!'

14

Cromwell Street Police Station, responsible for the area which included Albert Road, had worked swiftly and efficiently. When Hallam arrived at the scene of Dickson's death, and had introduced himself to the stout, red-faced sergeant in charge, he found all emergency measures set up and working smoothly. Two uniformed constables were stationed on the pavement at the gap between the houses, gently but firmly resisting the efforts of a small crowd of gaping, craning people who were trying to indulge morbid appetites by a closer look at what was going on. Dickson's body still lay on the trodden earth, but it was decently covered by a tarpaulin and around it a space had been marked off with ropes and metal stakes. Two patrol cars and an ambulance were drawn up to conceal the body from the street and a constable was in constant touch with the local headquarters through the medium of his portable radio. Hallam took it all in as he arrived, and turned to the sergeant, whose name was Merryweather.

'Excellent work, sergeant. You've done a grand job. Now put me in the picture, will you?'

'A woman rang from the box yonder, sir. Gave the location but it seems she cockled over before she could give her name. A passer-by saw her fall and managed to get a bit of sense out of her. He's standing by, ready to be questioned, the girl's in the end house there, being taken care of. Her name is Janice Kilburn. It seems she and the dead man were friends, she was meeting him here. She managed to tell me as much. There's a small confectioner's shop across the street and one of my chaps has picked up some story from them about a van driving off from this spot. There are some tyre tracks near the body which may prove useful.'

'Right. As soon as the photographers arrive — Ah, looks like them now. We'll get the pictures and then he can be moved.'

Spratt got out of the police car and came hurrying forward. He shook his head gloomily.

'Bad do, this, sir. Complicates the thing more than ever.' He nodded to the portly sergeant. 'Hallo, Fred.'

'So you know Sergeant Merryweather?' Hallam said. 'Good. We're working with him on this.' The uniformed sergeant's complexion flushed an even deeper red in gratified pleasure. Chief Inspector Hallam might well have put it the other way, that he, Merryweather, was to work with the C.I.D., so reducing him to a mere taker of casually-flung orders. He pulled down his well-filled tunic.

'I suppose you'll want to have a look at the body, Mr. Hallam? I did that myself, of course, before we covered him. Just to make sure he really had gone. No doubt about it, though. Shot at fairly close range, I'd say.'

'I'll see him in the ambulance, sergeant. The sooner we get him out of sight, the better. Set the photographers on, will you,

Jack? While they're busy I'll see this passer-by you mentioned, sergeant.'

Merryweather turned and beckoned and a small, hatless man who had been hanging about by the telephone box came forward, eager to talk.

'Banks, sir. Lionel Keith Banks. I live at 36 Albert Road here. Ice-cream vanman. Work for Kreemikones.'

'Right, Mr. Banks. And your story, please?'

'I was on me way home from work, see. And I'm coming up to the phone box when this girl rushes up to it and sorta plunges in. I see her dialling and speaking, like, and then, just as I'm passing, she disappears from sight. I stops and looks in and there she is in a dead faint on the floor. I gets her out and props her up against that low wall in front of the end house.' He started and blinked his eyes as magnesium flared. 'She comes round a bit and points over yonder. 'He's there — he's lying there!' she says. I nips across to have a look. My God! Well, I comes back and I asks her who she's called and she says just police so I rings for an ambulance as well and then I takes her into this corner house.'

'That's very clear, Mr. Banks. Now, did you see anything of a small van along Albert Road before you reached her?'

He shook his head. 'Not as I noticed. There was the usual traffic going by, of course.'

Hallam turned to a young man in a belted raincoat who had come hurrying up towards him. Merryweather, stretching out a huge hand, gripped the mackintoshed shoulder. 'Just a moment, you, if you don't mind. Clarion bloke, sir,' he said to Hallam.

'Ah, yes, Roberts, isn't it? No camera? That's good. No pictures at the moment, Roberts. And keep from under our feet, won't you? Here — meet Mr. Banks. He knows as much as I do. Take him into the pub across yonder and buy him a stiff drink. He needs one, and he's earned it. If you come back in twenty minutes I may have time to talk to you.

'The photographers should have finished, sergeant,' he went on, 'so we'll get the body out of the way. Will you see to that? You'll be able to supervise just where the ambulance men should put their feet better than I can.'

Merryweather nodded and bustled importantly away. Hallam stayed where he was, looking around him. Just a vacant space in the middle of Albert Road where a house clearance had been made. There was a wall along the far side with a door he knew gave access to Price's garage. On either hand the houses still standing were built out into small backyards, with outdoor water-closets at the end of them. Beyond these, a narrow alley and then the backs of the property in Willow Street.

Behind him, on the pavement, an excited murmur arose as the sheeted form on the stretcher was lifted carefully in. Hallam said, 'I'll just have a look at him before you go,' and one of the attendants switched the roof-light on, stepped in beside him and drew the covering blanket down.

Even in death the red hair flamed, the immature beard stuck out aggressively. Hallam shook his head sadly, briefly mourning a life cut so cruelly short in all its vigour and promise. He bent to examine the wounds as best he could; two holes, closely spaced, blasted into the chest. Small arm fire, of course. Ah, well, the doctor and the lab men would have all the answers.

'Take him away,' he said quietly, and sprang to the ground. The ambulance was started up, it backed away from the roped area, swung round and out into Albert Road, its bell chiming commandingly.

Hallam stepped forward. Spratt and an assistant were busy sketching, measuring, going meticulously over every inch of the ground. Merryweather's forces had just been augmented by five more constables, he was setting them to work on a search of the whole area. Hallam spoke to Spratt.

'I'm going to have a word with the girl. First house yonder, isn't it, Sergeant Merryweather?'

'That's right, Mr. Hallam. The house-holder's name is Duncan. Want me with you?'

'No, you carry on here.' He went back towards the road. Now the main actor of the drama had made his exit, the crowd was thinning, drifting away towards an evening pint, towards television, and eager, no doubt, to tell all and sundry, 'I was there.'

His knock was answered by a small rotund person, middle-aged, with that air about her which is usually called motherly. She smiled at him.

'Mrs. Duncan? Good. I'm Detective Chief Inspector Hallam. I'm told you have the young lady here who reported this business.'

'Yes.' She stepped outside the door and closed it gently behind her. 'Terrible thing to happen. State of shock, that's what she's in. I've put her in the front room and I switched a fire on for her and she has just managed to drink half a cup of tea.'

'I need to ask her a few questions, as soon as possible, Mrs. Duncan. Do you think . . . ?'

'I don't see why not, sir. I mean, she's got to face it sometime, hasn't she? Yes, you come in and have a go.'

She opened the door again and Hallam

followed her by way of a small hall into a room, clean and bright, where an electric fire was turned up to full strength. A tall, fair-haired, attractively-pretty girl was leaning limply back in a large easy chair, staring at the ceiling. She turned her eyes towards them, looking at them bleakly, helplessly.

Hallam signed for Mrs. Duncan to stay, she nodded understandingly and took a chair by the door. Hallam went forward to the settee in front of the fire. He began to speak gently, telling Janice Kilburn who he was, apologizing for having to trouble her, thanking her for waiting there to give him a chance to talk to her.

'I'll make it as brief as I can,' he said, 'and then we'll take you home and you can get some rest.'

His manner acted on the girl as he had hoped it would. She shook her head as if to clear it, wriggled her body like a dog coming out of water, and he saw some of the tenseness go out of her. She picked up the teacup by her side, drank and put it down. Her hands were reasonably steady.

'All right,' she said, and her voice,

though it was larded with the local accent, was pleasant enough. 'I suppose it'll all seem real someday. Just now it's only a dream — and I can't seem to wake up. Anyway, what do you want to know? I came to meet Gin — Gerry, that is, I found him lying on the ground out there, I thought he'd been taken ill and I bent down to see what was the matter. I — I touched him and my hands got all covered with blood. And somehow I knew he was dead. So I rang the police, and then I fainted.'

'Yes,' Hallam said quietly, 'and I'm afraid that's a scene you'll have to live through many times before you start to forget it. However, you will, in the end. Now I want you to try and tell me all about this meeting, when it was arranged, what you were proposing to do — every little detail.'

Janice took a deep breath. 'It was only this morning . . . ' Hallam heard of Dickson's call at the shop, of his insistence that Janice should meet him at this precise time and place. The chief inspector's gentle probing brought out the story of the friendship which had existed between the two young people. He gathered the impression that it was towards Janice Dickson had always turned when he was in need or trouble.

'Had he any enemies, do you know, Miss Kilburn?'

She was talking quite freely now. 'None as far as I know, but, you see, Gerry led his life at the university apart from me, if you get what I mean. Oh, he took me to dances there sometimes, but he never talked much about the place, or what he did there. Sometimes I wouldn't see him for weeks and then he'd suddenly drop in home and say how about an evening out? And we'd fix one up.' Her brows knitted. 'It's a funny thing, you know, about that. I mean, him ringing me up at business and saying I'd got to meet him tonight. First time he's ever done that, he always arranged meetings beforehand. And he sounded sort of scared on the phone. Almost — but I can't remember if I thought of this at the time or after — almost as if he was needing some protection.' She dashed the back of her hand across her eyes. 'He didn't get much protection from me tonight,' she said tremulously.

Hallam saw that the tears she needed were not far off.

'One last question, Miss Kilburn. Did you see anything of a small van driving away from that piece of ground?'

She shook her shining head. 'I can't — can't remember.' And then that head went down into her hands and Hallam got to his feet. 'Let us know when she wants to go home,' he murmured to Mrs. Duncan, who had also risen quickly. The woman nodded and went forward, her arms stretched out.

'That's it, my lamb, you have a good cry. It's all right, now, precious, it's all over . . . '

Hallam closed the door quietly upon them and left the house.

Sergeant Merryweather was waiting for him, holding the Clarion man, Roberts, on an invisible leash of bland officialdom. The reporter broke away and rushed up to Hallam.

'Chief Inspector! You promised!'

'I know. And Sergeant Merryweather here, having been in at the start, shall give you all the official facts.' Merryweather grinned, noting the emphasis on 'official.' 'By the way, sergeant anything new?'

'Nothing, sir. My chaps have combed the entire area. I've got the man from the shop across here. Sergeant Spratt's having a word with him now.'

'Right.' Hallam joined his own sergeant. Spratt indicated the stout, balding man at his side.

'Mr. Watkins, sir. Proprietor of the shop across the road. He saw a van turn out of here, just before seven o'clock.'

'Two minutes to,' Watkins said. 'I was stood looking outa me window, thinking about closing up. Started off quick, this van did, came off that waste like a rocket and went hell for leather towards town. Green Austin Countryman, two fellers in it. I didn't get any sort of a look at them, and I didn't take the number, of course. Why should I?'

'No reason at all,' Hallam agreed. 'Now, think hard, Mr. Watkins. Was there anything at all unusual about this van?

Any little detail by which, let's say, you could pick it out in a line-up of half-a-dozen green vans of the same make?'

He put the question merely as routine, without any hope of a positive reply. But Watkins nodded quite eagerly.

'Yes, there was something. See, I noticed it was an Austin Countryman because I used to run one myself till recently and when you've had a certain make of car, and you see one of the same sort, you take notice. Now, the jacking lug on my van broke off. There's one of these on each side of an Austin, you know, just under the door sills. The garage people said it wasn't unusual for them to go. It must have been hanging loose for some time before it finally dropped. And ever since, when I see a Countryman, I take note of the jacking lugs — if they're all right. It's a sort of habit I've got into. Sounds silly, I know.

'Well, now, see. The van came off this bit of land and swung across the road right-handed. That brought it close to where I was stood. So I could see well.

And the jacking lug on the near side was hanging down loose.'

'You could swear to that, Mr. Watkins?'

'I could.' He passed his tongue over his lips. 'Was it them in the Austin as did this job, then?'

'It's just possible. We know no more than that at present. We may have to trouble you for a formal statement.'

'Anytime you like, Chief Inspector. You know where I live.'

He nodded, and walked back across the road. Merryweather, having got rid of the Clarion reporter, joined Hallam and Spratt.

'Right, sergeant,' Hallam said to him. 'It'll have to be a house-to-house now. All round this empty piece and along the other side of Albert Road. We'll need extra men, so will you get on to Central and see what they can do for us?'

'Right away, sir!' He stepped away, moving swiftly, for all his bulk. Hallam, alone with Spratt for the first time that evening, grinned wryly.

'Well, Jack! What they call a right do, isn't it?'

'I'll say, sir. All of a piece with the others d'you think? I mean, this would be too big a coincidence to be an isolated job.'

'I agree. So we'd better get on to Patrick Molloy.' He glanced at his watch. 'There's just a chance one of those patrol cars can get him at home before he sets out for the university. If he is at home, or on the way to his usual work!'

'I'll see to it, sir. To H.Q. if they contact him?'

'Yes, There's not much else you and I can do here tonight. Merryweather'll clear up the odds and ends.'

The drizzle, which had eased off, returned with a sudden sweep of cold wind. Hallam was turning up the collar of his raincoat when a voice hailed him.

'Hey! You the chief policeman, then?'

He swung round, to be confronted by a small, wizened elderly man swathed in a thick cocoon of coat and muffler, a large cap almost hiding his features, and, on his feet, a pair of slippers.

'I suppose you could call me that,' Hallam replied pleasantly. 'You want to speak to me?'

'I do. You see, the wife's got a bit funny in her old age and she would have it I'd better have nowt to do with it. You get mixed up with that, she says, and one night a mate of these thugs'll bust in here and revenge himself on us both. Said she'd seen that done on the telly. Rubbishy stuff, telly is. But I know me duty as a citizen.'

'I'm sure you do, Mr . . . ?'

'Exley, sir. George Exley. Me and the wife live in that first house next to this opening.'

'Yes, Mr. Exley?'

'Tonight, about a quarter to seven it'd be, I had occasion, sir, to relieve me bowels. We have to go to the end of the yard to the water closet. I was sitting there when I heard a motor-car drive in and stop just beyond our wall. You know, folks have no right to bring cars there, there's a notice — '

'I know. We'll have to do something about it. So this car . . . '

'It pulled up and I heard a fellow say, 'You'll have to reverse and face the main road. We'll make a quick getaway then.'

So I could hear these gears grinding and messing about and then another fellow says, 'How's that, then?' and the first one said that'd do and then the second said, 'Think he'll be fool enough to turn up?' but I didn't hear what his mate answered. They started talking low and then the car moved a bit farther away and I come out and went into the house. Now the point is this. One of them fellows was foreign. Not the driver, he spoke Deniston. But the other one.'

'You mean he had a foreign accent? Not Irish, by any chance?'

'Oh, no. Proper foreign. He spoke English good but it was the way he talked. We've a lot of Pakistanis about here. Well, a bit like them, only different.' He jerked at his large cap. 'That's all I've got to say. I didn't see 'em, you understand.'

'You've been a great help, Mr. Exley. Now, you get back in the house out of this damp. We may have to have another chat with you later.'

The old man shuffled off and Spratt, who had returned to listen to part of the story, closed the notebook he had been using.

'So we've got this much, sir,' he said. 'Dickson shot at close quarters on turning up at a pre-arranged meeting. Two men, one possibly a foreigner, in a green Austin van — '

'With a jacking lug loose and ready to fall off.'

'Ah! Yes, that's something. We've got some good tyre marks, too.'

'Let's hope they help. At anyrate, Molloy doesn't seem to have been here, according to Exley's story. I'll just have a word with Merryweather and then we'll get back to H.Q. With luck, Molloy should be there.'

Molloy was there. They joined him in the interview room, and found the Irishman in an extremely disagreeable mood. As he pointed out to them, it was long after eight o'clock, and he should have been on duty.

'I persuaded the sergeant out yonder to let me ring in and tell 'em I'd be delayed,' he growled. 'But it's me that's never been late signing on at all. And what you would be wanting with me again, I can't be thinking.'

'Just a few questions, Mr. Molloy,' Hallam said. 'I'm sure you won't object to them. We have to ask them, in view of Gerald Dickson's death this evening.'

Molloy stared wide-eyed at them. 'Ye can't mean the lad Red Dickson?'

'I do. He was shot this evening on the piece of waste ground in Albert Road where you met him yesterday. Your story to us this morning wasn't true, of course.'

'Red Dickson, is it? God rest his soul!' He crossed himself devoutly and sighed. 'Ah, then, I did tell ye only half the truth this morning, but only for the lad's sake. He did a small job on me car, and he made a mess of it. He didn't want his boss to know, and I agreed he could put it right when I met him yesterday. And he's dead, so you're telling me!'

'Yes, Mr. Molloy, he's dead. And we're checking up on everyone who knew him. That's why I'd like an account of your own movements this evening.'

'Sure. I got up at five and had me meal. 'Twould be just after six when I left the house with me landlady's son, Timothy. I took him with me in the car to Garland's Gym in Heather Street. We go there every Wednesday. I need a good work-out once a week to keep meself fit. I did so tonight. Then I had a shower and a chat with the boys and I was just about to leave to drive on to work when the car police called, me landlady having sent them down there. And that's the holy truth.'

'It's an excellent alibi,' Hallam agreed gravely. 'And it leaves me with only two more questions. First, have you any idea at all who could have shot Dickson?'

'That I have not, then. Apart from what he did to me car, I hardly knew the lad, ye see.'

'Second question, then. What was in the note Dickson put through the letter-box at your lodgings today?'

Molloy's eyes flickered uneasily, but he answered readily enough.

'Ah, that, now! You'd been to see the lad and he was wanting me to know what he'd been telling you. So I wouldn't shoot off me mouth and get him in trouble at the garage.'

'You have the note still?'

Molloy shook his head. 'Sure, I put it in the fire when I'd read it. What would I want to be keeping it for?'

Spratt saw him out. When he returned to Hallam's room the sergeant glanced at his watch. Hallam nodded sympathetically.

'I know, Jack. But we'll be here some time yet, I'm afraid. Come on, let's get down to work with what we have.'

15

When Hallam reached his office on the following morning, Spratt was already there, leafing through a pile of reports.

'Morning, Jack. Have a good sleep?'

'A short one,' Spratt grunted. 'These are the house-to-house reports from Albert Road and Willow Street, sir. They're all in now. But there isn't a single lead in any one of them.'

He stacked the papers neatly and pushed them into an envelope. 'Ah, well, the day-men will be working on the garages by now. Perhaps they'll turn something up.'

'Let's hope so.' Before he had left for home on the previous night Hallam had put out an all-stations request. Today, as soon as the garages in the City of Deniston opened, police officers on beat would be visiting them with requests that notification should be given of any motorist bringing in an Austin van, green in colour, for a jacking lug replacement. The local Austin agents, who dealt in spare parts, had not been overlooked, either. It was hardly likely that a car recently involved in a killing would be brought to public notice in any way, but the task had to be undertaken, on the off-chance.

'There's the doc's report on Dickson, too,' Spratt went on. 'Two shots, close range. Bullets extracted and Ballistics have added a note that they appear to be Luger-type ammo. Which is nice to know but doesn't get us very far at present. Ah, yes. Something else. Message from St. Mary's Hospital. The accident victim there has recovered consciousness and may be able to make a statement soon. I've sent Whittaker along.'

'Good.' Hallam spoke absently, turning over the morning contents of his In tray. He pushed the tray aside.

'And how does our last night's theory look to you in the cold light of day, Jack?'

'Still reasonable, sir. Bradley was killed because he saw something he wasn't meant to see. He was waiting for

Humpkin, and strolled out to see if the man was anywhere around. What Bradley saw had some connection with the safe robbery which we've decided to consider the centrepiece, as it were.'

'Carry on. You're doing fine.'

'Young Dickson was involved in the said robbery. A diversion had to be staged to keep Hackitt, the nightguard, out of the way for a while. So Dickson fixed up the clock tower climb with his two pals. Hackitt — and remember, Dickson made sure they would be seen by him up there — would be bound to take care they got safely down, especially as he knew the lame lad, Shaw. Hackitt went round to where he knew they'd have to come down, right out of sight of the science department, as it was planned he would. After all, apart from any other consideration, it was his duty to get their names.

'And while Hackitt was out of the way, the science department was entered, the key to Peel's room was taken from the small office near the entrance, the safe was rifled, the key returned and the thief or thieves cleared off, closing the office, and the main door, behind them.

'To get in by the main door and into the small office, duplicate keys must have been already made from those Hackitt carried when he went on duty. He took them from a board in the head porter's office. They could have been removed at some time, kept long enough for impressions to be made. Matter of a few seconds. And this, sir, we decided, was where Molloy comes in. We know he has some connection with Dickson — that car-repair story was far too thin — and he could have taken the keys from the board easily enough. But we've not enough proof yet to charge Molloy — after all, there are other night-guards who could have done it — so all we can do at present is to watch him. Lowther's doing that job. He rang in just before you arrived. Molloy left the university this morning at his usual time, drove straight to his digs, and, it seems, has gone to bed. Lowther saw him at a front bedroom window in his pyjamas, drawing the curtains across.'

'Good. Now let's have the bit about Dickson.'

'They — and as secret papers were stolen and Dickson was a keen Communist, we might well guess who 'they' are — either decided Dickson wasn't of any further use to them or they thought he might break down under pressure from us. So he had to be eliminated. We can assume Dickson had some fear this might happen, since he insisted his girl-friend should be present at the meeting-place chosen. She arrived too late. And that's as far as we've got.'

'Yes,' Hallam said, 'it appears to hang together, but it could all be blown sky-high by Dr. Peel re-appearing and saying he'd taken the papers from the safe. I wish he'd surface again. We would know where we were a great deal better.'

'If he ever does surface,' Spratt began, and reached out for a ringing telephone. 'It's Whittaker,' he told Hallam. 'Back from the hospital. Will you see him now?'

Hallam nodded, and Detective Constable Whittaker came briskly into the room.

'It's Humpkin all right, sir. He was on his way to the university to see Bradley when he stepped off the pavement and was hit by a car. He's bought an old house in Thorndale which he's having modernized. The builders discovered a little boarded-up cubbyhole in the attic full of old papers. Parish records, Poor Law correspondence, and so on. Historically interesting, he thought. Didn't want to keep the stuff himself so got in touch with the Regional History people at the university here. Bradley got the letter he'd written and suggested a meeting. Humpkin was bringing the papers along to the said meeting so Bradley could examine them. He had them in a small canvas holdall with his night things, as Bradley was going to put him up. He was just asking what had happened to the holdall when a nurse came up and shoved me away, said the patient had talked too long already. Which was lucky for me because I didn't know about any holdall.'

Spratt exchanged glances with Hallam. 'Harlow Street, sir. That's where he was hit. Biggest percentage of sneak thieves in that district I've ever known. Somebody would whip it as he walked by, I'll bet, while Humpkin was still lying there. That's gone for ever.'

Hallam nodded. 'It's a detail we can't be bothered with now. I take it, Whittaker, that Humpkin won't be discharged from hospital just yet?'

'Not for some days, sir. I'm quoting the ward sister.'

When Whittaker had gone, Hallam got up from his desk.

'Back to the university now, Jack. We'll have a look at Dickson's room. It's high time we did. If we hadn't finished so late last night — What's wrong?'

Spratt had snapped his fingers and was now busily rooting among the papers on his desk.

'Contents of Dickson's pockets, sir. Almost forgot to mention it. Usual items, except there was no wallet, no pocket diary, and no keys.'

Hallam spoke as he moved to the door.

'So he was probably searched after he'd been shot and anything likely to be incriminating taken from him. That's all right, but I don't like the no keys. Bound to have one at least, for his room.'

They wasted no time on the way to Monkbridge House and hurried along the corridor to Dickson's room. The door was locked.

'To be expected, of course,' Hallam muttered, and looked up as the door next to Dickson's opened and a tall, handsome young man, dark-haired, wide-shouldered, stepped out into the corridor. He looked at them unsmilingly.

'Can I help you?' The question came out abruptly.

'Yes, sir, you probably can.' Hallam returned his unwinking stare with a brief, pleasant smile. 'We are police officers, and we're here on a very sad errand, I'm afraid.'

The other nodded, without relaxing the tenseness of his attitude and bearing.

'You mean — Red Dickson? It was in the papers this morning. You say you are police officers. May I see your warrant cards?'

Hallam turned his head towards Spratt. The sergeant dug out his card and handed it over.

'Detective Sergeant Spratt, Deniston

C.I.D. Right.' The card was handed back. 'And you, sir?'

Hallam gave his rank and name. The young man's features softened.

'Sorry to be so suspicious, but I had to check, especially after what happened — oh, less than ten minutes ago. In fact, I was wondering if I should ring the police. Here, you'd better both come into my room, I think.'

It was a duplicate of Dickson's quarters, where they had been the previous day. Their host settled Spratt on the bunk bed, gave Hallam a chair and remained standing, his back to the window.

'My name is Merrill,' he began. 'Anthony Merrill. I'm doing Social Studies. Second year. Dickson, as you know, was my next-door neighbour. Naturally, his death — it's been a shock.'

'You were intimate friends, Mr. Merrill?'

'By no means, Chief Inspector. To be brutally frank, I didn't care for him much. His ideas and interests were just about diametrically opposed to my own. But as neighbours — sharing neighbours as the expression is here — we got on extremely well together. Which was fortunate.'

He stepped forward to open a door.

'You see, each pair of rooms here has the toilet and shower in common, and it could be possible for sharing neighbours to get in each other's hair quite a lot. Dickson and I never did this. Incidentally, if you want to get into his room, you can do so through my toilet entrance. The doors don't lock, they have bolts on the outer side. If you don't want your neighbour barging in on you by way of the toilet, you slip your bolt in.'

'You mentioned something which happened this morning, sir.'

'Yes. I had a late breakfast in the dining kitchen at the end of the corridor here. I'd learnt of my neighbour's death by then. I came back here and went into the toilet to brush my teeth. I heard somebody moving about next door, there was the snapping sound the bed lockers always make when you close them.

'I thought it might be one of your chaps having a look round, in view of

268

what had happened. In which case he'd probably want a word with me, so I decided I'd get it over, and I went through. Well, this chap certainly wasn't a policeman. He was short and squat, with thin grey hair. I'm sure, as I pushed the door open on Dickson's side of the toilet, he jumped away from the bed lockers. I asked him who he was — he'd got in by the corridor door, of course — and he said he was an electrician, checking up on the heating thermostats.'

Merrill swung round and pointed. 'This thing under the window, with the grille, is the central heating unit. And this numbered turn-switch by the window is the thermostatic control, so everybody can have his room just the temperature he wants. Of course, we're always getting workmen around, as this is a new building and there are a few creases to be ironed out yet. But this chap was wearing gloves! Close-fitting, thin leather gloves, not new. He saw me looking at them and said he'd better get to work and he took the gloves off and opened a bag with electricians' tools and equipment in it. He started to fiddle with the thermostat and I left him to it.

'But I listened hard, because by now I was very suspicious of him, and though I didn't hear any more lockers opened, I was waiting when he came out of Dickson's room and I asked him to come and look at my thermo. One of the retaining screws was loose and I hadn't a screwdriver. He said he hadn't time but I insisted that it wasn't a minute's job. I said if he didn't attend to it I'd go back with him to the foreman and report he'd refused to do an essential job. So he came in and tightened this screw, which I'd loosened, by the way, with my penknife. To get at it he had to move my transistor set out of the way. It has a smooth metal case which I'd wiped carefully over before I'd purposely set it on the windowsill next to the thermo.'

He grinned boyishly. 'I should stop reading thrillers, I suppose.'

'You may have done a marvellous job of work,' Hallam said warmly. 'Let's go next door now.'

Dickson's lockers had indeed been

hurriedly searched. The papers, books and miscellanea they held were flung together anyhow. Merrill shook his head.

'Dickson never left them like that. He was one of the neatest men I've ever met. Tidiness was an absolute fad with him. If I hung my towel the least bit askew on the rail in the toilet, he'd straighten it. All his stuff was kept in meticulous order.'

'So we'll wrap up your transistor carefully, take it away with us and hope for the best,' Hallam said. 'But before we do, is there anything else you can tell us?'

Merrill nodded. 'I think there is,' he said.

16

'Yesterday morning,' Merrill continued, 'I answered the phone out there in the corridor. A man's voice asked to speak to Dickson. I didn't think he was in, but I checked on that. I told the caller so and he left a message with me for Dickson to call Mr. Smith as soon as he got back. I was asked to tell Dickson it was urgent he should do so. As soon as my neighbour returned I gave him the message. He looked, and sounded, upset when I mentioned Smith's name.

'He didn't go to the telephone immediately — went into his room for a few minutes. He came out again just as I was leaving here for lunch at the refectory. Now, I must admit to a piece of unpardonable curiosity. The call I'd taken had intrigued me rather and I was tempted to hang around and listen to Dickson talking into the phone. But I couldn't do that, of course.'

'You say the call you took intrigued you, Mr. Merrill. In what way, exactly?'

'The caller wasn't English. He had a foreign accent but I've no idea of his nationality. His way of speaking was, well, aggressively contemptuous, almost, like some big business tycoon giving orders to an underling. Dickson wasn't the type who'd normally stand for that sort of thing and I was surprised he knew anyone who would have talked to him like that.'

'This is all most helpful,' Hallam said. 'You're sure you can't pin down the accent more accurately?'

Merrill shook his head. 'I was surprised that a foreigner should give the name of Smith, though,' he added.

'We'll have to see if we can find him.' Hallam grinned at Spratt.

'There are over five hundred Smiths with telephones listed in the Deniston area,' he said gloomily. 'And it doesn't follow this man was using his own telephone. It could easily have been someone else's.'

Merrill said, 'The telephones in this building are all automatic. You don't have

273

to put in a call through a switchboard operator. When I left this room to go to lunch, Dickson had just picked up the phone and I saw the first number he dialled. It was a two. Then he moved slightly and covered my view of the other five numbers he dialled. And now I've told you all.'

Hallam rose and thanked him. 'We'll take your transistor set and we'll check on that electrician,' he said. 'If he was a phony he probably used a key to Dickson's room which was taken from your neighbour's body after he was shot. I suppose there are duplicate keys to these rooms?'

'Yes, in the office downstairs.'

They went to the ground floor and found no duplicate key had been borrowed by any workmen that morning. They checked with Maintenance and the chief electrician there settled any remaining doubts. There had been no complaints of faulty thermostats, none of his men had been working in Monkbridge House that morning, none of them fitted the description of the man who had searched Dickson's room.

They returned to Headquarters and Spratt took the wrapped-up transistor set to Fingerprints, pointing out that this was a hurry-up job. Fingerprints were not impressed. All their jobs were hurry-up ones.

Hallam found the transcript of a message from Sergeant Merryweather on his desk. A woman constable had been sent to see Janice Kilburn, who had not gone to work that day. She was still very shaken but she had been able to give one piece of information.

'The girl said Dickson did not talk much to her about his university friends,' the message ran. 'But, some time ago, when he had just begun his second year there, he mentioned a Mr. Leng a number of times. He seemed quite proud to know this person. Then he stopped talking about him altogether and when Miss Kilburn asked about him once, Dickson became evasive and shut her up very sharply. She does not think this could possibly be of importance to you, but she felt she should give you every detail.'

Hallam rang for Whittaker. 'Get hold of the local telephone directory and make a list of the Smiths therein with phone numbers beginning with the figure two, will you? Let me have the list as soon as it's complete. Come in!' he added to a knock on the door.

'There's a man called Lister outside, sir,' a constable from the main office reported. 'He found a jacking lug from an Austin van this morning.'

'Send him in!' Hallam looked towards Spratt. 'Keep your fingers crossed. Things may be moving at last.'

Lister was a cheerful, extroverted young man. He wore a white coat with 'Regal Dairy Co.' emblazoned on its top left-hand pocket and he carried a peaked cap in his hand.

'Wilfred Lister, sir.' He settled himself in the chair Spratt brought forward. 'Milk delivery roundsman, employed by this lot.' He touched the name on his pocket. 'This morning, while I was doing Cunliffe Street I picked up this.' He took out a dirt-encrusted object and reached forward to place it on Hallam's desk. 'Must have dropped off a car, I thought, but I couldn't just place what sort of a part it was, and being curious, I bobbed into Moody's garage in Ribble Road as I was passing it. Thought Bob Moody might tell me. He said one of your chaps had been in this morning, asking about such a thing. Bob said it was off an Austin van, and he advised me to report it at once. I was just on finishing the round, so I did that and came straight here with it. Seemed the best thing to do.'

'It certainly was, Mr. Lister.' Hallam got up. 'Cunliffe Street, you said. Let's have a look at this wall map.'

Lister's finger stabbed at the large-scale street plan almost at once. 'Here's Cunliffe Street. I was going towards Westbourne Avenue and I found the lug just about here. You think it's the one you're looking for?'

'It could well be, Mr. Lister. We'll follow it up. I expect you get to know the locally-owned vehicles on your round fairly well. Does a green Austin van ring a bell to you?'

Lister shook his head. 'Only one of

them I know belongs to a mate of mine. And that's a grey 'un. No, sorry.'

He was asked for his address, thanked and shown out.

'Do we call the jacking lug inquiries off now, sir?' Spratt asked.

'They should all have been done by this time. Let's leave it, just in case. Ah, Whittaker, what luck?'

'Just eleven Smiths, sir, with figure two starting numbers. Here they are, with initials and addresses.'

'Bring your list over to the street plan here. Now, let's assume one of these Smiths has an Austin van. He's driving from his place of residence to Albert Road by way of Cunliffe Street. Puzzle, find the appropriate Smith. I'll leave you to it. Yes, sergeant?'

Spratt had been answering his telephone. He grinned widely.

'Fingerprints, sir. They've got some lovely dabs on the transistor set. And these, beyond doubt, were deposited by our old friend and peterman, Benny Clegg.'

'You don't say! And he told Bert

Hackitt he'd retired from crime. Getting too old for it. The big stuff, yes, but as Bert said, the university job was the sort Benny could do in his sleep. We don't know yet if he did it, of course, but he's mixed up in this lot somehow. So have him pulled in, will you? I'm beginning to have a faint impression we might just be starting to get somewhere. How's it going, Whittaker?'

'Shan't be long now, sir. I've eliminated five of them.'

'Knock off for a minute. We've earned ourselves a cup of coffee.' Hallam produced a florin. 'Fetch us three from the canteen, will you? Sergeant Spratt likes his black — white for me.'

Whittaker, returning, met Spratt at the door of Hallam's office. The chief inspector put down one of his telephones as they went in.

'Lowther just reporting. Nothing doing at Molloy's. I've arranged for a relief. What, no spoons, Whittaker?'

'Sorry, sir. Forgot 'em. Brought sugar and no spoons! I'll slip back — '

'Don't bother.' Hallam opened a

drawer. 'We'll use this. It's quite clean — I think.' He produced a wooden paper knife, designed like a miniature police truncheon, except that it was flat. There was even a tiny leather thong looped to the handle.

'Christmas present,' he said. 'Time it was used for something.' He sugared his coffee, stirred it, shook the drops from the paper knife and passed it to Spratt. The sergeant looked at it thoughtfully and then spoke slowly.

'I wonder if they issue anything like a policeman's truncheon to those security guards at the university? I'm thinking of the doctor's report on Bradley. Before that smoothing iron was used on him he was struck with a blunt-ended weapon. Worth checking?'

'Every time.' Spratt picked up a telephone and was put through. He made his inquiry, listened, and replaced the receiver.

'Nothing doing there, sir. Uniforms and reinforced caps only.' He drank his coffee moodily.

Whittaker had finished his drink and

had gone back to his task. Now he turned away from the wall.

'This is the best bet, sir, I think. Smith, M. K. Tobacconist and Newsagent, 14 Eastwood Road. Care to look, sir?'

Hallam and Spratt joined him.

'Say he wants to get to Albert Road from home, sir,' Whittaker explained. 'He's got two main routes, either down Eastwood Road into Victoria Road and so through City Centre, or else cut across country, as it were. Which is a shorter, and a quieter, way.

'To do that he goes along Eastwood Road and turns into Swan Street. Off that by way of Lincoln Avenue and so on to Albert Road. But, look. A man who knew the Eastwood Road district well would cut off down here to get to Swan Street. Save himself half a mile.'

'I see. And your 'down here' is Cunliffe Street, where the lug was found. That's very good Whittaker. We'll all go to see Mr. M. K. Smith. Tell the desk, will you, sergeant, that if Clegg is brought in he is to be kept here till we get back?'

The mid-morning traffic was not heavy

and Eastwood Road was barely two miles from police headquarters. Inside ten minutes Hallam and Spratt were walking into the small shop which carried 'Mark K. Smith' on its fascia board. Whittaker had been left with the car in a side street.

Smith's place of business was a typical example of the policy of small profits and quick returns. Besides tobacco and newspapers he sold confectionery, paper-backs, stationery, greeting cards, aspirins, toilet paper and corn paste. In all, he probably made a fair living.

The man behind the counter was about middle height. He had a large nose and deeply-set eyes in a long narrow face. His hair was a dusty brown, greying over the ears. He looked at the two detectives with a shopman's alert, questioning air.

'Good morning, gentlemen.'

'Mr. Smith?' He nodded, and Hallam went through the routine of self-introduction. The proprietor's brow furrowed and there was an immediate tightening of his thin mouth. Hallam noted the signs but did not overrate them. They were often to be observed when a plain-clothes man announced himself.

'What's up, then?' The question was jerked out.

'We've a few questions to ask you, sir. Shouldn't take a minute. Just routine, you know. Do you own a green Austin Countryman van?'

'No.' He rubbed the back of his hand swiftly across his mouth as if to wipe away the explosive negative. 'I mean, yes. I had one, but somebody either borrowed it or knocked it off last night.'

Hallam and Spratt stood aside as a man came into the shop for cigarettes. Smith seemed to welcome the interruption. He took a long time to find change from the till.

'Y'see, it's like this,' he said when the customer had gone. 'I keep the van in the yard, back of the house and shop. It's an open yard. Of course, I lock the van at nights. It wasn't there this morning. I mean, car locks, well, they're nothing to thieves these days.'

'You've reported the loss?'

'I was just going to when you come in. I've been busy this morning.'

'Was the jacking lug loose on the near side?'

'Not as I know. What is all this, anyway?'

'We'll get to that in a minute. Do you know a university student, Gerald Dickson, generally known as Red Dickson?'

'Not me. But I read the Clarion this morning. He was shot in Albert Road last night, wasn't he?'

'Yes, and it's possible your van was used in the shooting, Mr. Smith. When did you see it last?'

'When we closed last night, at six. I didn't go out of the house again, nor did the wife. You mean somebody pinched the van and used it for this shooting?'

'Possibly. You say you didn't know Dickson, so it wasn't you who rang him up yesterday morning at Monkbridge House, where he lived?'

Smith's headshake was emphatic. 'I certainly didn't.'

'Did anybody else use your phone yesterday morning?'

'Not as I know of. The wife never touches it. She's rather hard of hearing and can't make much of a phone conversation.'

'And you are the only two in the house?'

Smith's tongue came out to pass over his lips.

'Well, there's our lodger, Mr. Leng. But you can't ask him, because he's out at business and I don't know when he'll be back.'

Spratt had been idly examining a stack of magazines on a side counter. He turned slowly at Smith's mention of his lodger's name.

'Fair enough,' Hallam was replying cheerfully. 'But we want to clear up what could be a misunderstanding as quickly as we can. So where can we find Mr. Leng?'

Smith shrugged. 'Look, he's a sort of general manager and accountant for a number of these Chinese restaurants. He goes from one to the other. I don't know where he'll be just now.'

'Leng,' Hallam repeated. 'Is he Chinese?'

'His dad was. Mother was English, I believe.'

They bade Smith good morning and

returned to their car. Whittaker was given instructions to watch the shop and look out for an Anglo-Chinese. If the man appeared, he was to be brought in at once for questioning.

17

Earlier that day, Arthur Howard had arrived at Kings Cross in comfortable time for the morning express to Deniston. He had spent a memorable evening with his friend Nick Glover, he had slept well and breakfasted excellently. True, there was a faint shadow to spoil a feeling of complete wellbeing, for, on arrival, he would have to report a failure of mission, in person this time. Though he'd been ordered to drop the Peel job, in the eyes of his superiors, no doubt, he would still be typed as having fallen down on it.

But worrying paid no dividends. He bought a paper and a sports magazine, chose a second class compartment and prepared to kill the return journey as pleasantly as possible.

The station clock at Deniston Central was just moving on to one-ten when he gave up his ticket at the platform barrier. He had had no lunch, but the station refreshment bar was handy. He was angling in that direction when he saw Dr. Peel making his way towards the main exit.

Jettisoning the thought of food, Howard turned to follow, convinced it would pay to keep the scientist in sight. It could ease matters for himself considerably if he were able to report Dr. Peel back at the university, or at home. It appeared Peel wasn't proposing to use a taxi; the exit to the rank was not the one he was taking.

Howard's self-imposed task proved a simple one. Dr. Peel made his way directly to the municipal bus station and to the departure stand used by the Northwood buses. When the bus arrived, Peel chose a downstairs seat while Howard went quickly upstairs. He sat at the rear, where, by peering over the guard rail at the head of the stairs, he could see the reflector, angled to give a view of the platform.

Peel, it seemed obvious, was on his way home. As the bus moved off, Howard wondered if he himself were justified in thus wasting his time by sticking to the man. Better perhaps to have gone directly to Headquarters to report what he had seen. But better still, he argued silently, to be able to say definitely that Peel had returned to his own home.

Peel rode to the Northwood terminus and strode away in the direction of Churchill Road. There were very few people about and Howard, though compelled to keep some distance in the rear to avoid recognition, had no difficulty in maintaining contact. Peel turned down Churchill Road, past the four new houses already occupied near the corner, past the still unbuilt-on field beyond them, to his own isolated villa. Howard strolled along behind him, hands in pockets, head bent, the perfect idler.

Peel entered the drive of his house. Howard watched him step into the porch, try the handle of the front door. Locked, Howard noted as Peel began to feel in a trousers pocket. But he hadn't found his key when the door was flung open. Howard saw Peel's head jerk back in astonishment as he was confronted by a powerfully-built, dark-haired man who wasted no time in words. He thrust out a hand, gripped the front of Peel's shirt and jerked him inside with a mighty heave. The door was slammed shut again.

'Wow!' Howard said softly to himself, and wondered what he'd tumbled into. Mrs. Peel entertaining a friend who was extremely annoyed because her husband had turned up unexpectedly to spoil things? But a married woman's bit of extra didn't usually answer the door. 'This I must see more of,' Howard decided and, turning through the gates of Ashlea, hurried up the drive. If things turned out to be normal in that house, after all, he had an excuse for calling. The police wanted Dr. Peel to get in touch with them. So he was the policeman bringing that message.

There were no signs of life in any of the rooms at the front of the house. The back door was at one side. Howard turned towards it, stepping quietly along the concrete path which led to it. He glanced into a large-well-appointed kitchen through a partly-opened window. Nobody there.

He went on round to the far side of the house.

Here, french windows of a lounge gave on to a large back garden. The windows were closed and curtains were drawn across them. That was odd, for there was no sun to spoil carpeting or upholstery. Howard went cautiously forward, stepping over a half-finished path of crazy paving which stretched out from the house.

There was a narrow gap between the curtains. He hesitated, not wishing to be caught peering into a room of a private house. Then from inside the room he heard a woman's voice shrill out in a scream of anguish and his hesitation vanished. He edged forward and took a quick glance into the room.

A short, squat man was grasping a young woman with fluffy fair hair, holding her with one of her arms pulled behind her. Both of them had their backs to the window. Peel was being forced through the door of the room by the big dark-haired man. The scientist's jacket had been pushed off his shoulders, pinioning his arms. He was struggling gamely but fruitlessly. Using a knee and both hands, his assailant was propelling him forward with little trouble to himself.

Howard dodged out of sight after that split-second glance. The situation was obvious and it was up to him to take over, fast. He ran back the way he had come and quietly tried the kitchen door. It was locked. So was the front door. But there was a bell-push. He set his finger to it, reminding himself that surprise was the only tactic here.

The human organism is not equipped to ignore endlessly a continuously-ringing doorbell. Howard knew that, for a while, the intruders would not answer the high shrilling he himself could plainly hear. They would hope the caller would go away. But in the end, somebody would have to answer the door. The smaller man had the woman — Mrs. Peel, of course — in a firm hold. He wouldn't want to release her. The other chap would have to do the door-answering, which meant he'd likely knock Peel out first. A pity about that, but it couldn't be helped.

Howard heard footsteps coming through the hall. The door's latch-lock was slipped, the door snatched open. The big man glowered at him. 'What the hell . . . ?'

He saw the blur of Howard's stabbing fist just too late. The blow, with Howard moving forward and using every ounce of his weight, caught him squarely in the solar plexus. He jack-knifed forward, grunting, and Howard put a right jab solidly to his chin. The man staggered back into the hall and Howard followed him, his fists finding their marks with the accuracy of the practised boxer he was. When, with a crash of his head against the newel post of the stairs, his man went down like a tipped cartload of bricks, Howard knew he was down to stay — long enough to leave for a brief spell.

He licked split knuckles, leapt over the fallen man and shoved his way into the lounge. A quick grin flashed across his face as he took in the situation. Mrs. Peel had freed herself and her captor was hunched forward, clasping his middle and retching violently. Her husband was sitting on the floor, feeling the back of his neck, his head moving muzzily. And Mrs. Peel, now snatching up a heavy bronze figurine from a side table, was in the act of bringing it down on the skull of her former captor when Howard jumped forward and grasped her wrist.

'You'll probably kill him if you do that,' he said.

'I was hoping to.' The fluffy-haired woman relaxed and smiled at him. 'You're not another of them, are you?'

'I'm a police officer, madam.' He had a grip of the still-gasping man now. 'I'd better tie this up. Have you . . . ?'

'In the kitchen. A plastic clothes line. I'll get it.' She put the figurine down. 'That's his gun on the table. Don't let him grab it.'

She helped Howard to tie the small man firmly into a chair, and being assured by the detective that he could manage the one in the hall, knelt down to minister to her husband. Howard took the rest of the clothes line, turned the unconscious man outside over on to his face and fastened his wrists to his ankles with knots which were well and truly tied.

Then he telephoned his headquarters.

Dr. Peel was recovering fast when Howard rejoined the party.

'We've met before, I think,' he said. 'Briefly, at Golders Green.'

'That's right, sir. But you take it easy now.'

'Yes,' Mrs. Peel said, 'and I'll do the talking. If I don't I'll probably have reaction-hysterics.

'That horrible creature' — she pointed at the glaring captive — 'arrived this afternoon with his personal thug. I opened the door to their ring and they pushed me inside. The thug produced this.' She thrust an arm behind her husband and brought out a solid rubber cosh, lead weighted, the shape and size of a police truncheon. 'He threatened me with it. They bundled me in here and demanded some papers which they said my husband would keep here, dealing with his research work. I told them I knew nothing about these, but I'm not a very good liar and they didn't believe me.

'So our friend here took out his pistol and began to talk about a smashed kneecap — to begin with. But then somebody — my husband as it turned out — tried the handle of the front door. The thug went to deal with this. He returned with Lewis, and then the front door bell began to ring and went on and on. The thug went to the door, having taken care of Lewis by a chop at his neck. I managed to wrench myself free. I stamped on one of Sonny Boy's feet and brought up my knee hard into his — well, where it would hurt most. My mother taught me that trick. As she used to say, there are times when a woman has to forget she's a lady. The rest you know.' She rose to her feet. 'A cup of tea wouldn't come amiss, I think.'

They had just begun to drink it when the two police cars arrived. Sergeant Spratt was in one of them. He stepped into the hall and bent to examine the now-struggling, cursing captive there.

'Take it easy, Molloy,' he advised. 'You're going to have lots of time to indulge in language. And who may this be?' he asked as Howard led the way into the lounge.

'Actually,' Mrs. Peel said, 'the thug called him Mr. Leng. Would you care for a cup of tea, Sergeant Spratt?'

18

On his return with Spratt from interviewing Smith, the tobacconist, Hallam had found a message awaiting him. A green Austin van, with a jacking lug missing had been reported, abandoned, at the edge of one of the municipal rubbish dumps near the Deniston city boundary. The local police division were towing it in.

'Smith's, without a doubt,' Hallam said to his sergeant, 'but that can stand over for now. Our job is to pick up Leng. It's lucky Janice Kilburn recollected the name. Makes a nice tie-up with Dickson. Will you get the operation moving?'

'Yes, sir.' Spratt went out to the main office. He was back within a few minutes. 'Okay, sir. And Benny Clegg's here. Very virtuous and indignant, I understand. In the interview room.'

'He can cool his heels there while we get our lunch, Jack. Twenty minutes more won't hurt him. Come on.'

They returned from the canteen to face a small, grey-haired man who sprang up at their entrance in outraged protest.

'Look here, Mr. Hallam, I gotta complaint. 'Tisn't right and 'tisn't legal, to treat me like this. I ain't bin charged — '

Hallam waved him down. 'Listen, Benny. You haven't been charged yet because, between ourselves, I'm in a bit of a difficulty.' He paused, staring blandly into the old lag's furious eyes. 'You see, I don't know whether to make it house-breaking, burglary — or murder.'

The fire went out of Clegg. 'What the 'ell d'ye mean?'

'Housebreaking.' Hallam ticked the items off on his fingers. 'At Monkbridge House this morning. Burglary, at the Science Department in the university, the night before last. Murder, same night. A man named Bradley.'

Clegg wetted his lips. 'I never heard such a load of rubbish — '

'You shouldn't have touched that transistor set in the room next to Dickson's,' Hallam cut in smoothly. 'Your dabs are all over it. Dickson, I should perhaps remind you, was also killed.'

'I 'ad nothing to do with any killing. I swear it! Look, Mr. Hallam, it's me own fault for touching a job what was beneath the dignity of a perfessional like me. Only, you see, the money was good, and I ain't as young as I was.'

'Tell it all to Sergeant Spratt, Benny. He'll charge you with the burglary job and when you've got it all off your chest we'll have it typed out and you can sign it.'

He went back to his office. There was no news yet of Leng, the detectives watching Molloy's lodgings and Smith's shop had nothing to report. There was still no word of Dr. Peel. Things were moving, but not fast enough, not smoothly enough, for his liking. Maybe, when Clegg had coughed . . . He picked up the receiver of a ringing telephone to learn that the Austin van had furnished no clues.

Then Spratt came in, buoyant and smiling.

'Got just what we want, sir. Benny says

he was contacted by a man in a pub. A stranger, according to him — the usual story. He was told there was an easy job, well-paid, for him. He decided to take it on and so met Molloy.

'Molloy told him a stunt had been arranged by one of the students to keep the security guard out of the way long enough to do this job. Molloy had keys for the outer door of that block and of the small office inside. He took the key of Peel's room, and Benny claims that he himself opened the safe in forty seconds flat. Molloy cleared it out, they locked all up behind them again and Benny scarpered. He'd had half his price, he was to get the rest last night, in the same pub, at a quarter to eight. Molloy turned up there, told him something had gone wrong and gave him orders to search Dickson's room today. He wouldn't wear that at first but Molloy said he'd better — or else.

'Dickson's key was delivered at Benny's lodgings early this morning. He swears he had nothing to do with the two killings, and I believe him. We're holding him, of course.'

'So Molloy was in it, after all, as we suspected? We'll disturb his slumbers at once, I think. Let's just check our facts. Molloy didn't shoot Dickson. He didn't drive the car to Albert Road. We can charge him with robbery, on Benny's evidence. Let's say the Anglo-Chinaman shot Dickson — remember old Exley, the pensioner, who heard a non-English accent? Dickson, I think, was getting scared and had to be eliminated. Right. We want the van driver, too. Smith, do you reckon?'

'Could be, sir. He wasn't happy when we were chatting him up this morning.'

'We'll get him down here to identify that van. And while he's here — ' His desk telephone rang.

Spratt saw Hallam's face, as he listened, assume a look of surprise, then of unalloyed satisfaction.

'Excellent,' he said. 'I'll send Sergeant Spratt and a squad car along there at once.'

He put the receiver down, expelled a deep breath and grinned widely at Spratt.

'How's this for a break, my lad?

Howard has Molloy, who must have dodged our man — slipped out the back way, no doubt — and another fellow at Peel's house. The good doctor is also of the company. I'm sure they would all love to have you join them!'

* * *

The Vice-Chancellor's room at Deniston University was spacious and elegantly furnished. Hallam and Dr. Lewis Peel sat in club chairs with Sir Vincent Wakefield, the Vice-Chancellor, between them. A secretary had brought sherry in delicate glasses, its arrival emphasising the informal, off-duty character of the meeting. Vaguely, Hallam missed the familiar presence of Spratt, who had not been invited.

The Vice-Chancellor, a tall man with a shock of thick grey hair and classical features, turned to Hallam.

'Well, Chief Inspector? We know the outline, but we need a fill-in.'

'Yes, Sir Vincent, and I'll be brief. The central motive was the theft of Dr. Peel's papers. It was hoped they would contain matters of supreme interest to the people for whom Leng was working. As he is half Chinese, the inference isn't difficult.

'Leng was here as a student. He got to know Dickson, who was proud of his communist principles. He also made the acquaintance of Molloy, in whose background, I fancy, there is a strong anti-British influence. And Smith, who was Leng's landlord and who agreed to help him at a price.

'Molloy obtained keys to the Science Faculty block, by taking Hackitt's keys from the board, ostensibly by mistake, and making impressions of them before he returned them. We've a witness who saw him return the keys to the board. Dickson's job was to divert Hackitt while the safe was being cleared. I imagine he was well paid for this, though no doubt he felt justified in acting for the sacred cause of communism.

'Clegg opened the safe. The papers they took were useless, but this wasn't obvious to Molloy. He handed them over to Leng, who was waiting out of sight of the scene of operations.

'Bradley, wandering round in search of Humpkin, saw Molloy do the handing over. Leng decided Bradley must be eliminated, so Molloy was ordered to silence him.

'Molloy followed Bradley back to his room. He was able to get behind the archivist and use the cosh he carried. The mounting iron was there and Molloy tried to confuse the issue and make a proper job at the same time.

'But the papers had proved worthless to Leng, and Dickson, we think, couldn't stomach Bradley's murder. He was almost ready to talk, so Leng and Smith met him in Albert Road and made sure he didn't. The bullets which killed Dickson have been proved to have come from Leng's gun, though Smith talked his head off about that job to us. And that, I think, is all.'

Sir Vincent inclined his head. 'Very concisely put, Chief Inspector. And now, Peel, over to you.'

'Yes. Well, of course, I was never fool enough to keep important papers in that ancient safe, though members of my staff seemed to think I did. I had such material, but my wife was the only person who knew where it was kept. There is a partly-made crazy-paved path in my garden. A rust-proof metal box is sunk under one of the slabs of that path. I can divulge this now because Security Executive in Whitehall will, in future, be responsible for any work I commit to paper. I made arrangements with them yesterday.' He looked at Hallam with a smile. 'I couldn't very well turn up at the Ministry with two detectives round my neck, you know, Hallam. Besides, I was not prepared for explanations just then.

'And now I have to reveal a personal matter which is of the utmost importance to me.'

Sir Vincent bowed again. 'We shall listen, and forget, Peel.'

'I had a sister who became mentally ill. Not to put too fine a point on it, she went out of her mind. This happened some eight years ago, before I met Hazel, my wife. Early in our acquaintance I found she had an inordinate fear of madness. I saw to it she knew nothing about my sister. We hope eventually to have children, but, had Hazel known of my sister Laura, she would never have dared . . . The heredity factor, of course, though I felt sure there was no fear of this.

'Laura was in Dr. Jamieson's nursing home and I visited her whenever business took me to London.' He sighed. 'Poor thing, she never knew me. On Monday afternoon, as I was looking over my notes for that evening lecture which I had taken home previously, Jamieson telephoned me. Laura had become seriously ill and had not long to live. I rushed up there, telling my wife some story to account for my journey. I had hoped to stay at Charles Mitchell's place, but everything started to go too fast all at once. I know it sounds absurd, but I didn't seem to get time to ring my wife as usual. Laura was already dead when I reached London. Though there was no need for a post-mortem, with Jamieson's help I persuaded a brain surgeon to do one. He found, as I had always suspected, that the insanity was due to pressure on the brain resulting from a head injury she had suffered as a young woman. She could have survived no operation to remove this pressure.

'I attended the funeral and cleared up what business matters I could. I had avoided the detectives and hoped to get home and tell my wife the whole story before I again became involved with the police. Instead of that . . . well, you know the rest. Leng was after those papers, and, if he had started to work on Hazel as he threatened, I'd have told him where they were. And what man would not? We owe a great deal to Howard, you know, Hallam.'

Sir Vincent reached for the sherry decanter.

'I insist on a stirrup cup. But before we drink, please enlighten me on two points. Why didn't poor Bradley tell Dr. Kirk, or Clift, about his late meeting with the Humpkin man?'

'We'll never know that,' Hallam replied, 'though we may conjecture Bradley wanted to handle the entire business himself and present it later as a fait accompli. The holdall containing the material Humpkin was bringing has never turned up. It's not likely to now.'

'And my other point. What will happen to Leng and his works?'

Hallam smiled broadly. 'That's a headache for Special Branch, sir. He's off my patch, and they can have him with my blessing.'

The Vice-Chancellor filled their glasses and raised his own.

'A worthy sentiment, to which I think we might drink, gentlemen,' he suggested.

THE END

Other titles in the
Linford Mystery Library:

THE CRIMSON RAMBLER

John Russell Fearn

The murder at Darnworth Manor was particularly baffling. Autocratic financier Warner Darnworth had been working alone in his study. The study door was locked on the inside, and the only window was of the non-opening variety. Yet Darnworth had been found slumped over his desk, shot through the head. No weapon was found, either in the room or anywhere else in the manor. To add to the problems of Chief Inspector Gossage and Sergeant Blair, every member of Darnworth's family had good reason to hate him.

ENFORCER

Sydney J. Bounds

When ex-Vietnam veteran Washington T. Diamond quits working as racketeer Leon Greco's 'enforcer', he and his nightclub singer girlfriend Chelsea are drawn into a web of danger. Greco exerts a vicious reprisal, but Diamond receives support from Cave, a police detective, who sets him up as a private investigator. But Cave is only using Diamond as a pawn to bring down Greco's empire. Diamond becomes the bait when Greco takes out a contract on him, and he needs all his jungle experience to stay alive . . .